Married to the man she met at eighteen, **Susanne Hampton** is the mother of two adult daughters, Orianthi and Tina. She has enjoyed a varied career path, but finally found her way to her favourite role of all: Medical Romance author. Susanne has always read romance novels and says, 'I love a happy-ever-after, so writing for Mills & Boon is a dream come true.'

Also by Susanne Hampton

Unlocking the Doctor's Heart
Back in Her Husband's Arms
Falling for Dr December
Midwife's Baby Bump
A Baby to Bind Them
A Mummy to Make Christmas
Twin Surprise for the Single Doc
White Christmas for the Single Mum
The Doctor's Cinderella

Discover more at millsandboon.co.uk.

MENDING THE SINGLE DAD'S HEART

SUSANNE HAMPTON

MILLS & BOON

First published in Great Britain 2019
by Mills & Boon, an imprint of HarperCollins*Publishers*
1 London Bridge Street, London, SE1 9GF

Large Print edition 2019

© 2019 Susanne Panagaris

ISBN: 978-0-263-07855-8

MIX
Paper from
responsible sources
FSC™ C007454

This book is produced from independently certified FSC™ paper to ensure responsible forest management. For more information visit www.harpercollins.co.uk/green.

Printed and bound in Great Britain
by CPI Group (UK) Ltd, Croydon, CR0 4YY

To everyone who has ever had their heart broken, only to pick themselves up, dust themselves off and find their *new* happily-ever-after.

And to my amazing new editor, Victoria. It has been a pleasure getting to know you…
and I truly love your work!

CHAPTER ONE

DR JESSICA AYERS paused for a moment to secure the weighty oversized handbag slipping from her shoulder. She needed to gain some level of composure before she stepped from the thirty-six-seat twin-propeller plane that had just endured a somewhat bumpy landing at Armidale Airport. The landing, however, was the least of her concerns, since 'bumpy' was on a par with the rest of her life anyway.

Drawing a deep breath to fill her lungs, she attempted to quell the rising anxiety she always felt when she arrived in unfamiliar surroundings. Constantly moving to new places was by her own design, but it still unnerved her a little and gave her an overwhelming sense of déjà-vu. One that she feared would never end. Another town. Another short-lived new beginning. In six weeks she would move on again.

Her willingness to fill in for local paediatricians on leave across the country allowed Jessica to move regularly around Australia. There was never time to plant roots or get comfortable. And that was how she wanted it to be, because neither were in her plans. Not any more. The idea of long-term in any part of her life was gone. Badly hurt, and carrying a level of shame for loving the wrong man, Jessica had decided there was no such thing as a happily-ever-after for her. She was now a rolling stone. Gathering no moss and with no ties to anyone.

And falling in love again was definitely not going to happen. It only brought heartache. And Jessica didn't want any part of that. Not ever again.

She doubted she was strong enough to survive another disappointment, unlike her best friend, Cassey, who seemed to rush back onto the online dating scene after each failed relationship. And there had been many. Jessica wasn't sure if that had compounded her opinion about men and love but it didn't matter. She was over it all. She knew for certain there was no good man in her future, only heartache waiting to happen if she travelled that road again.

Jessica was not an optimist like Cassey.

She glanced up into the overcast sky. It was close to five o'clock on a June afternoon, it was blowing a gale and the cloud-covered sun was beginning to bid farewell to the cold winter day. She held onto the rain-dampened handrail with her woollen glove and quickly realised that was not the best idea. Now her glove was wet. With a sigh, she took the seven steps down to the ground, collecting more droplets of water as she held on tightly. The wind pushed and pulled at her and she struggled to keep her steps in line as she slipped off one soggy and one dry glove and made her way over to the pile of small carry-ons assembled under the wing of the plane. Space restrictions in the tiny overhead lockers meant none of the bags had been allowed in the cabin. Jessica's was easily recognisable from the pool of small black bags and quickly she reached down and wrapped her now bare and cold fingers around the handle of the compact silver hard case that matched her other luggage. She had always liked the things she could control in her life as it helped to have a sense of order. It was a trait passed down from her father, a military man. It was a pity that was not how she lived any more. Nothing much in her personal life bore much semblance to order.

She attempted to brush away the thick wisps of her hair blowing haphazardly across her face, almost obstructing her view as she walked across the windy tarmac. Still deep in thought, Jessica put one foot in front of the other as she fought hard not to be blown away by the fierce breeze that had made their landing jerky. Her jacket had blown open and the wind cut through her thin sweater as she avoided the puddles of water. Armidale's chill was nothing like the muggy Sydney weather she had left behind.

Silently she questioned with each of her considered steps what she was doing. Not the last hour, taking the flight, nor last month, accepting another temporary Paediatric Consultant position, ironically covering the resident paediatrician's honeymoon, at Armidale Regional Memorial Hospital. No, instead Jessica wondered what she was doing with her life. Her lips wilted at the corners the way they always did when she allowed disappointment in herself to creep back. But a moment's pity was all she would allow. She couldn't afford to fall in a heap because there was no one to pick her up.

She only had herself. Her parents had both passed. Her father had died when she was sixteen and her mother three years ago. As an only child, Jessica had no siblings to turn to now, only cousins and friends, but they were all either settling down and having families or travelling the world *before* they settled down, married and had a family. And Jessica didn't even have a boyfriend, nor would she ever again. Marriage wasn't in the stars for her. She'd thought it was, she had even wandered into wedding gown boutiques to gaze at the stunning white lace and satin creations hanging in rows and pictured which one she would wear when she walked down the aisle to Tom, the man of her dreams.

She had always imagined a flower girl and a pageboy and a stunning bridal bouquet of white roses and a quaint church with the setting sun shining softly through the stained-glass windows. And her groom waiting at the altar, where they would hold hands and make a commitment to love each other for the rest of their lives. But not any more because trust was the foundation of marriage and Jessica didn't trust men. They lied, they made promises they couldn't keep and they broke hearts, sometimes more than one at a time, with their actions.

Biting the inside of her cheek, Jessica dragged her bag into the small terminal. With no romantic dreams, she had to make the best of what she did have and that was a six-week placement in a hospital in the middle of country New South Wales. She'd not worked in a rural city or large country town, and Armidale had been referred to as both. She tugged hard on her bag to lift it over the slight step. It wasn't a particularly heavy bag, as her shoes, clothes and other belongings were packed into her checked luggage; she was just taking out frustration on an inanimate object and potentially using more force than was logically required. Just as the wind outside had been doing to her. Jessica Ayers was being a little unnecessarily rough. It was that simple. She wasn't as patient as she had once been with people, and definitely not with awkward carry-on-sized suitcases.

The weather outside had made her feel as if she had flown in on a broomstick but she knew she would settle in a day or two. She always did. Adapt to her new environment but not stay long enough to get close to anyone— that had been her modus operandi for close to a year. It was getting more difficult each time and Jessica had begun to admit to herself that she was growing tired of running. Now she was facing yet another new beginning that wouldn't change a thing or bring her close to being the person she had once been: an optimistic young doctor who loved life and thought she had found the man to love her as much as she loved him.

It had been twelve months, and her heart was still numb and her mind racked with shame for almost tearing a family apart. A family she knew nothing about. She couldn't come to terms with what had happened, nor could she settle her feelings and, as a result, herself geographically. Was she the victim? Or the perpetrator? She still wasn't sure. But the one thing she was sure of was the need to keep moving. Although the disappointment she felt still followed her wherever she went. Disappointment in the man who had deceived her and deceived his wife. And disappointment in herself. She no longer trusted her own judgement.

The idea that she had been the *other woman* tore at her core. Upsetting thoughts about herself and how she should have known better had a way of creeping into her mind and pitching a tent. She felt physically sick when images of Tom making love to her crept back into her mind. The man who, unbeknown to her, had a wife and children waiting at home for him. Each time she moved town she hoped the change of scenery and distance from Sydney, where he was still playing happy family, would hasten some level of amnesia around her actions or perhaps just help her to find acceptance that she couldn't change what had happened and allow her to move on. But that was yet to happen.

Dr Jessica Ayers would spend the next six weeks in a country town where she knew no one and no one knew her. Armidale was not her forever. It was just another stopover, a place where she could hide from the rest of the world until she knew what she wanted to do with her life. A life that would never have the happily ever after she had once thought she had all wrapped up with a perfect bow.

Jessica accepted there was no fairy tale ending for her. She would only have herself and her regrets...and the wish that one day she could learn to trust herself again.

But she doubted that would ever happen.

'Oh, God. Oh, no.' Lost in her maudlin thoughts, Jessica didn't notice, until she felt the bump of her carry-on bag landing on the ground, that she had run over the man's foot as she had struggled to get inside the terminal building. Looking down, she noticed the highly polished leather loafer with a damp imprint of her wheels. 'I'm so sorry—I didn't see you.'

'It's fine,' the deep voice comforted her, adding, 'I'm pretty sure nothing's broken.'

She looked up to see the stranger's lips curve to a half smile. She couldn't help but notice his vivid blue eyes harboured a smile too. Jessica doubted that her actions would have brought about his reaction. Running over someone's foot could not ordinarily incite a happy response. No, this man looked like someone who had found a bowl of cream and had been swimming in it. His happiness was palpable but she wondered how deep it ran. A new love affair, perhaps? His looks would no doubt have most women swooning. A player with his choice of women to keep that smile firmly secured on his chiselled face, she surmised with absolutely no evidence. She didn't need hard cold facts. Dr Jessica Ayers was ready to judge then quickly hang, draw and quarter each and every man who crossed her path. But, despite her misgivings about the male population, including this stranger, she knew he deserved an apology.

'No, really, I'm sorry. I should've been more careful.'

'Accidents happen. Honestly, don't give it another thought,' he told her with that same smile that once again made his blue eyes sparkle like sapphires against his lightly tanned skin. Perhaps the happiness wasn't a mask. It was emanating from somewhere deep inside. Resonating from his core, his very being, and it was the most genuine smile that Jessica thought she had ever seen. No, not thought, knew. Jessica had never before seen a smile quite like his.

Without saying another word, he walked away, leaving her standing alone and a little stunned, breathless and wondering what on earth had just happened. Looking down at her feet, she shuffled nervously as she tried to bring herself back to reality. And gain some perspective on the situation. A man about whom she knew nothing except he was handsome and had stylish shoes, now with an unfortunate wet tyre imprint from her bag, had taken her breath away.

Why would she be reacting to a complete stranger that way? Or any way? She should have dismissed him as she did all men, but she hadn't. It didn't make sense. There was something different about him. Perhaps his reaction, perhaps something else. She wasn't sure. Edging closer to the baggage carousel, Jessica was a little confused about why she was giving the man more than her usual thirty seconds of considered disdain. Her curiosity about the source of his happiness lingered in her thoughts. It didn't seem put on; it seemed so real.

The call for passengers travelling to Sydney to make their way to the departure gate suddenly brought her back to reality with a thud. The reason for the man's happiness wasn't her concern. She had enough on her plate without thinking about anyone else. She needed to collect her luggage and make her way to the real estate office to collect the keys to her rental. It would be a tight timeline as the office closed at five-thirty. But she couldn't help but watch him walk over to the other side of the small terminal along with the other passengers. She told herself it was her need to find the luggage carousel and not curiosity that had made her eyes follow him. Gingerly she made her way there too. Looking around, Jessica saw families hugging, reunited lovers kissing and a few like herself standing alone with no one to greet them.

There was no one waiting to greet him either.

That she kept noticing him was beginning to irritate her. She assumed it was because he was the first person she had spoken to since arriving at her new temporary home and the first man she had run over with a suitcase. She was definitely overthinking everything she decided and purposely looked away.

Within moments an array of suitcases, predominantly black with an occasional colour variation dotted among them, and oversized backpacks began to push their way through the grey rubber flaps and onto the carousel. A pushchair appeared and even a surfboard. The terminal was too small to have a separate oversized items area. Quickly her fellow passengers retrieved their bags while still chatting to their companions. One by one they began to exit the terminal. She spun around and found the handsome stranger had gone too. She wasn't sure why, but she wished he was still there. Strangely, his disappearance made her feel alone again.

Jessica pulled her concentration back to the job at hand. Finding her bag and doing it quickly so she wasn't homeless that night. With concern mounting, she watched as the carousel emptied one case at a time until there were none in sight. And no one still waiting empty-handed like her. Her stomach fell as she moved closer to the rubber slats. She peered through to see no more bags waiting to emerge. Anxiously her eyes darted about as she chewed the inside of her cheek again. It was becoming a habit she knew she had to shake. Looking out to the tarmac through the expanse of floor-to-ceiling windows, Jessica could see the bags for the next flight out of Armidale being loaded into the plane. The same plane in which she had arrived. It was a one plane airport. There was no more luggage being taken off. She had to accept her bags had clearly never made it onto the plane in Sydney. Or they'd made it onto another plane heading for God alone knew where, the idea of which was far too upsetting for Jessica to consider at that time.

The only possessions she had with her were the contents of her handbag, her laptop and some notebooks tucked inside her carry-on.

A rising sense of loss surged through her and almost brought her to tears. She had no belongings...not even a toothbrush...nothing and no one in the world belonging to her.

Jessica was once again reminded that she was alone. In a strange town far from the place she'd once called home.

Dr Harrison Wainwright stepped from the Armidale Airport terminal and into the now darkening car park. It was cold and crisp, the way he liked it. He had sorely missed the clean fresh country air. It was still damp from a light shower before they'd arrived and that made it even better in his mind as it more readily carried his favourite scents of hay and eucalyptus. He paused for a moment to fill his lungs like a man who had been starved of oxygen. Winter in Armidale was his favourite time of year and he didn't try and mask his happiness. Los Angeles was not his type of town at any time of the year and six days breathing air heavy with smog was six days too many.

With the *Sydney Morning Herald* newspaper he had picked up at the airport that morning tucked under one arm, he steered his suitcase to the cab rank. Harrison was conscious of the lightness of his steps, despite having just had his foot run over by the pretty stranger inside the terminal. Perhaps more than merely pretty, he mused. Beautiful was closer to the mark, he decided as he allowed his mind to slip back momentarily to when he'd noticed the emerald hue of her eyes, the softness of alabaster skin and ash blonde hair that skimmed her shoulders. The windswept curls that framed her heart-shaped face.

But there was something behind her eyes that struck him and played on his mind as he waited for the cab. She was stunning in an almost hauntingly sad way. A little lost. She was not from around the town he called home. She must be travelling through or visiting.

He pushed the image of her face and the questions he had about the purpose of her travelling to Armidale from his mind. He was not going there again. Curiosity about a beautiful stranger in his town had completely changed the course of his life once before. And almost ruined it. Not to mention threatened his sanity over the years. He would never let himself travel that path again. He was finally closing that horrendous chapter and was ready to move on. It had been five years of something close to hell but he had emerged and would never let his heart rule his head again. He was finally happy… Well, his new version of happy.

With his chin jutted in defiance he waved down the cab that was approaching and banished the stunning stranger's face from his mind. Finally, he was back home with the outcome he had so desperately wanted. And nothing and no one was going to steer him off course again.

With the custody papers in hand and the signed divorce papers on their way to him in the coming days, he would soon be officially a free man. It was as if a burden he had carried for so very long had disappeared overnight. Nothing could make him happier than the knowledge that now he could move on without the possibility of one day losing his son in a custody battle. No threat of his son living across two continents. No arranging proposed maternal visits that never eventuated. No more explaining to the five-year-old boy why his mother promised to visit and never did. He could finally look into his son's innocent blue eyes and know Armidale would be their forever home. And Harrison Wainwright was determined to be the best single dad possible.

He pushed away the surge of anger that threatened to ruin his victory. He had what he wanted and he had to let the hurt and broken promises go. He was determined to release the sadness and disappointment that had consumed his waking moments for years. But

Harrison was a realist and he knew it would take time.

Being in a relationship would never again be an option for him. From that day forward, it would just be Harrison and Bryce. There was no need and no room to invite anyone else in their lives. His house and his heart were full.

And he would never risk his son being hurt again.

CHAPTER TWO

'EXCUSE ME, MISS. Can I help you?'

Jessica was so preoccupied she didn't hear the male voice behind her. The empty luggage carousel mirrored her life more than she cared to acknowledge. The fact there was nothing to see consumed her attention. The sound of the aircraft engine starting finally forced her to glance over to the thirty-six-seat plane taxiing down the runway in preparation for take-off into the stormy early evening sky. Her missing bags meant she would not be sleeping in her favourite pyjamas that night. And that was assuming she was able to collect the keys to her rental property and actually had a bed for the night.

It was all a little overwhelming and she wasn't entirely sure what she was going to do. That had been a regular state of mind for a while and completely out of character from the old Jessica. She had always known what to do, even as a teenager. Forget having a social life, she had her head in her textbooks, even on weekends. She'd excelled at school every year until the final year. Then she'd graduated top of the class with perfect end-of-year examination results that saw her in the top twenty students across the entire state of South Australia, which meant her higher education study preference of a medical degree was guaranteed along with being presented to the Premier at Government House. Straight out of school, Jessica Ayers had been on her trajectory to becoming Dr Jessica Ayers, Paediatric Consultant. She'd considered specialising in paediatric surgery and did head down that path and gained the skills but, after a year of surgical study, she'd decided that it was the interaction with children offered by the Consultant's position that made her the happiest.

Over the years there had been few boyfriends to distract her. No jam-packed social calendar to compete with her study schedule. Nothing to prevent her from achieving her lifetime goal. Including her vision, from her very first day in medical school, of one day being Head of Paediatrics at a large teaching hospital. Jessica Ayers had been an unashamed planner.

But there were some things in life she couldn't plan. Some things had just occurred without any decision-making by Jessica. Some of them were very sad, such as losing her father while she was still in high school so he never saw her graduate from medical school, and then losing her mother when she was thirty. At least she was grateful that neither had witnessed her fall from grace in dating a married man.

Now she was flying by the seat of her pants in regard to everything and anything…and she wasn't very good at it.

'Miss, I asked if I can help you.'

Jessica turned her attention to the uniformed older man standing behind her; his bomber-style jacket was emblazoned with the Armidale Airport logo.

'My name is Garry; I'm with the airport.

I'm assuming you're still waiting here because your bag, or bags, didn't arrive?'

She feared her distracted state might have given the appearance of being dismissive. She felt sure she was on a roll in managing to offend her adopted new town's population one person at a time. Damaging one man's foot and being plain rude to another.

'Bags—there's two of them—and I'm sorry, Garry, I didn't mean to be impolite.'

'Think nothing of it. You seem a little frazzled. Have you been on a long haul flight and then a connection to get you here? A handful of our passengers came in today from Los Angeles. The Armidale Romance Writers group attended a conference in the US and four of them just came back. My sister-in-law is one of them, that's why I know, and one of our doctors was over in America as well, not that he attended the romance conference,' he said with a wry smile. He added, 'It's a country airport, what can I say, there's not much gossip that gets past the ground staff here.'

'Well, I haven't flown too far at all. I've just done fifty minutes from Sydney so I definitely

can't blame my poor manners or distracted
state on jet lag...'

'You might not have done a long-haul trip
but missing bags is a stress all of its own, so
let's see if I can help.'

Jessica wondered for a moment if she had
entered some parallel universe. Was this town
in country New South Wales the friendliest
place on earth? This man was being so kind
and helpful, just as the man, whose face was
still etched on her mind, had been so gallant
about her clumsiness. Immediately, she pushed
away the image she still had of the first man,
the one she'd run over, but she knew it was
more than his appearance that was lingering.
There was something about him that was not
easy to forget, for some strange reason. But
she had to do just that. She had to find her
bags and get to her accommodation or face
being homeless.

'It's been a long day and I have to get to the
realtor by five-thirty to get the keys to my
rental property...and I have nothing except
these,' she told him tilting her head in the di-

rection of her carry-on and her handbag that she was holding up.

'I must apologise that the rest of your bags didn't arrive. It doesn't happen too often, I must say, but that doesn't help you. If I can have your name I'll start the process to find them.'

'Dr Jessica Ayers,' she replied.

'Nice to meet you, Dr Ayers,' he said as he reached for the extended handle of her carry-on bag.

'Please call me Jessica.'

'Certainly, Jessica. Let's get you over to check-in,' he said, pointing to the other side of the terminal. He added, 'I can get some more details and chase the bags up for you. If you can give me the baggage receipt that was issued with your boarding pass, I'll call through to Sydney and make sure that your bags are sent here on the next flight, which is at eleven-thirty—'

'That's late but at least there's another flight coming in tonight,' Jessica cut in with a faint strand of renewed hope colouring her voice. Excitedly she handed over the documents he requested and then followed him from the departure and arrival lounges and in the direction of the main entrance.

The man's brow wrinkled as he shook his head from side to side and with it swept away Jessica's hope of a swift solution.

'Unfortunately, your flight was the final one from Sydney today. There next one arrives at eleven-thirty *tomorrow morning* and I can have your bags couriered to your home,' he said as he maintained a fast pace. He was a man on a mission and that gave Jessica some small level of comfort as she kept up with him.

'My home? I have no idea if I'll have one. I think my deadline to pick up the keys from the realtor is just about to pass.'

He raised his wrist and glanced at his watch as they reached the check-in counter. 'It's five-fifteen but a cab can have you into Armidale in ten minutes. Let me make a call to the agent and ask them to stay back in case you're a few minutes late getting there.'

'Do you honestly think they will?' she asked, confident that in her home town of Sydney there would be somewhere between a fat chance and absolutely none that they would actually remain open for her. Their care factor about her having to find accommodation for a night would be around about the same—zero.

'Do you have the business name?'

'There's more than one in town?'

Garry smirked and shook his head. 'Armidale is actually a rural city and we have hot running water, traffic lights…and more than one real estate agent.'

Jessica felt quite silly. 'I'm sorry.'

'No need to apologise. You're obviously a big city girl. Is this your first visit here?'

Jessica nodded sheepishly as she scrolled through her emails on her mobile phone until she found the realtor's name. 'Dunstan Boyd is the property manager—' she paused as she squinted to read the fine print in the signature block on the email '—at…'

'Boyd and Associates Real Estate,' Garry finished her sentence.

Jessica dropped her chin a little and stared up at him curiously. 'You know them?'

'Yes,' he told her. 'My sister-in-law works there. Not that I thought you'd have any trouble anyway, and we do have some nice motels in town if there was a problem, but I can almost guarantee she, or one of her colleagues, will stay back and you won't be homeless.'

Jessica drew breath and then emptied her lungs just as quickly with relief at Garry's announcement. While she had nothing to wear and she would have to wash her underwear in the basin and dry it over the bath, she would at least have somewhere to do that.

'Now, if you can give me your contact details, someone from the airport will call you tomorrow and arrange to have your bags sent to you when they arrive.' He pulled a pen and paper from the pocket of his bomber jacket.

Jessica took the pen and paper and scribbled down her mobile telephone number, which he then tucked back in his jacket pocket as they walked outside to the cab rank.

'It might be best sending them to the Armidale Regional Memorial Hospital,' she told him as she tugged her jacket up around her neck. The air was even colder than when she'd alighted from the plane. 'I'll be there so they'll be no one at home to collect them, that's assuming you're right and I have a home.'

'You'll have a home, Jessica. Don't worry.'

There was an empty cab already there and no one else waiting. Garry opened the rear door of the cab for Jessica and she quickly climbed in the back as he leant in the open front window and spoke to the driver.

'Can you please take this young lady to Boyd and Associates Real Estate, Twenty-nine Marsh Street.'

'Sure.'

Flooded with a relief she'd thought impossible ten minutes previously, Jessica put the window down. 'Thank you so much,' she said as the cab pulled away from the kerb.

'You're very welcome.'

Garry was right; his sister-in-law's colleague didn't mind staying back and the cab driver waited while she rushed inside. The young man asked her for identification, had her sign two documents and then gave her the house keys and the keys to the rental car that had been left that morning in her driveway. Jessica had arranged for everything to be in the one place, and it was a glimpse of her previous attention to detail. Although twelve months ago she would have shipped clothes ahead and arranged for the local dry-cleaner to press and hang them in her closet and have the pantry and refrigerator stocked with low-fat food. The kind that Tom liked. Tom, the womanising, cheating bastard whose cholesterol levels she had worried about for the better part of a year.

But, thanks to said two-timing low-life, the Jessica of late was nowhere near that organised when it came to her personal needs. On the job, though, she hadn't changed. She was as dedicated and focused with her patients as she had ever been.

'Call me on my mobile if you have any questions. It's a nice little house, clean, tidy and fully furnished, as you saw in the photos. I think you'll like the street.'

Jessica was not about to be fussy. A bed and bath was all she needed right now, and a car for the morning to get her to the hospital.

'I'm sure it will be great and thank you again for staying back for me,' she said as she held on tight to both sets of keys as if they were her lifeline.

'Not a problem, happy to help.'

Half an hour later, with two bags of groceries on the back seat, the cab pulled up in the front of the darkened house. The amiable cab driver from the airport pick-up had kept the meter running while Jessica had signed the lease and picked up the keys, then stopped for milk, bread, oatmeal, fresh fruit and other staples, including bubble bath, a toothbrush and toothpaste from the small grocery store that stayed open until ten o'clock every night.

Her new role began bright and early the next day so she wanted to have a nice home-cooked dinner and an early night, followed by a reasonable breakfast. She knew that she would hit the ground running and had no idea if she would get a lunch break so needed to be prepared for a long day on her feet on the wards and potentially even in surgery if required. In a smaller hospital the roles and duties were sometimes less defined and far broader in nature than in the city hospitals and she had the surgical experience if called upon.

Jessica took a brief study of the street as the cab turned in. It was tree-lined and had a simple prettiness about it. Very country, she mused silently as she noticed the houses either side of the one she would call hers for the next six weeks were softly lit from the inside. Lights and probably open fires, she thought. Curtains were drawn but the glow could be seen from the street.

Jessica's new temporary home had nothing to signify life at all. She wasn't surprised. She couldn't expect anything more than that. It wasn't as if she knew anyone in town; there would be no one there to welcome her to the new house. It had been the same wherever she had been posted but generally she chose apartments close to the city hospitals to avoid the harsh reminder every night that she was arriving home to an empty place.

She still had her terrace home in Surry Hills, an eastern suburb of Sydney, that she kept as a base but, since Tom had spent two or three nights a week there during their year-long relationship, she chose not to actually live there any more. She would fly in and out and collect her belongings between assignments. One day she would sell it but she hadn't set a time frame for anything much in life.

Jessica was just glad that she had a key to her rental home and would soon be soaking in a hot tub. The thought of steaming bubbles infused with lavender brought a much-needed calm to her.

The cab driver pulled the carry-on from the boot of the car as Jessica made her way up the driveway, pulling her coat up around her ears against the bitterly cold air. The sensor light switched on as she approached the front porch, showing her the facade of her accommodation. It was very homely and looked freshly painted. It was grey with white shutters and a red wooden front door. Either side of the red door was a topiary tree in a square cement pot and in front of the door was a mat emblazoned with *Welcome*. She was relieved to see the small hatchback rental car was parked under the carport, as she had requested. The colour matched the front door. The garden was simple but sparse with mostly lawn and an edge of low native bushes. There was nothing that looked demanding of her time and that also made her smile. Jessica was not a green thumb so took comfort in the fact she could just engage with a mowing service a few times during her stay and leave the rest to Mother Nature.

'I can take it from here. Thank you,' Jessica said as she put the key in the door. Turning back to the cab driver, she gave him cash to cover the fare and a little extra.

'Are you sure you don't need me to help you get everything inside? You have shopping too.'

'No, I'm fine to do it myself but thank you for offering.' Her response was genuine and ingrained. She could manage on her own. She didn't need a man to help her. Jessica Ayers was more than capable of taking care of herself, despite everyone being so kind since she'd arrived. The friendliness of the locals was almost making her feel at home. Under different circumstances, in another lifetime, she might have even thought it would be a lovely place to live. But everywhere was temporary to Jessica now.

The driver nodded, put the fare in his pocket and, blowing warm breath on his cupped hands, walked briskly back to the cab. Along with not needing his help, Jessica hadn't wanted to delay him any longer. They had chatted during the brief trip and she had discovered it was the end of his shift. He was heading home to his wife and newborn baby boy after he dropped her off and she appreciated he had already waited for her to do the shopping.

With the front door open, the light from the porch illuminated the interior of the house enough for Jessica to find the inside light switch. She quickly found out the freshly renovated house was as simple and tidy inside as it was out. And there was a faint hint of fresh paint and furniture polish but neither were overpowering.

'New start for us both, hey,' she muttered as she carried the shopping bags inside and closed the door on the cold night air and went in search of a heater, a bath and her bed.

An hour later Jessica emerged from the bathroom with her freshly washed hair piled inside a makeshift white towel turban. The central heating had warmed up the house while she had been under the shower. She had decided a soak in a bubble bath could wait as she saw there was a hairdryer in the first drawer, along with samples of shampoo and conditioner, and clean hair might distract from the clothes she would be wearing on her first day on the job. And, much to her joy, she had found a thick white bathrobe folded on her bed. Nice touches, she thought, and decided to make good use of all of them.

If at least her hair looked clean and tidy she hoped everyone might overlook the fact she was wearing jeans and a sweatshirt. Thank goodness it wasn't summer as the T-shirt she wore underneath was a gift from the plumbing service that replaced her hot water tank and their marketing slogan—*If you want clean pipes, look no further*—would not have been well received. Ordinarily she would never have travelled in such casual clothes, let alone considered going to work in them, but she had been pushed for time to get to the airport that afternoon and decided to stay in the clothes she had been wearing to run errands in the morning. And with the missing suitcases and no shops open, other than the grocery store, she now had no choice.

Jessica walked around the house and found it was clean, tidy and had a nice ambience to it. The furniture had character, as opposed to some of her previous rentals that had generic flat-pack-style furniture that had an impersonal motel feel. This house was homely and had recently undergone a freshen-up. All the furniture was in good condition but eclectic in style and age and she suspected it had belonged to others before it came to rest there, and that felt nice. A country home filled with furniture that came with history. One that she assumed would be country-style sweet, not sordid, as she considered her history to be.

Brushing aside thoughts of her past, Jessica made herself dinner and washed the dishes by hand. There was a dishwasher but it would have been a waste to turn it on for one dish, one glass, a knife and fork and two small pans.

Besides, she had nothing much to do other than dry her hair and head to bed. She didn't have to spend any time at all deciding what to wear on the first day of her new job—missing luggage had seen to that.

'Are you going away again, Daddy?'

Harrison closed the story book and gently put it on the nightstand beside the bed as he looked down lovingly at his son snuggled next to him. 'No, Bryce. Daddy's not going anywhere.'

'So, when I wake up you'll be here? You won't get on a plane and go away again?'

The innocent questions tugged at Harrison's heart and he knew immediately he'd done the right thing in fighting for custody. For the right to keep his son safe in Armidale with those who loved him. Those who had since the day he was born. And always would.

'I'll be right here when you wake up and then I'll take you over to Granny and Grandpa's house.'

'For breakfast?'

'For a second breakfast, as Granny always

likes to make something special for you before school,' Harrison said as he edged off the bed and, pulling the covers up to Bryce's ears, he ruffled his thick black hair.

Bryce giggled. 'I hope she cooks pancakes.'

'I do too,' Harrison said as he kissed his son's forehead, turned off the light and walked quietly from the room, safe in the knowledge that Bryce was right where he needed to be... and nothing and no one would ever put that at risk again.

The alarm clock ensured Jessica woke on time and found her underwear had dried on the coat hanger she had hung on the shower rail. The house had remained toasty warm overnight and she felt unusually relaxed as she lay under the warm covers surveying the room in the daylight that was creeping through the gaps in the heavy curtains. The walls were a very pale blush, so pale that she hadn't even noticed the night before and had thought it to be cream, but now she could see the hint of colour. It was also in the bedspread and the throw cushions that Jessica had placed on the armchair the night before. There were two framed prints, both of birds, and the furniture was made of oak, including the bedhead.

For a rental, it was quite lovely, she thought as she climbed from under the covers. She could have slept in a little longer as she had over an hour before she was due at the hospital but, as always, she wanted to arrive early. She also wanted to call the airport and remind them to send her bags to the hospital the moment the plane touched down, so she could change into something more suitable as soon as possible.

A quick shower and an equally quick breakfast of oats with blue gum honey and a cup of tea followed by an equally quick phone call to the airport saw Jessica lock the front door of her home thirty minutes later. She had checked directions on her phone the night before. When she rented the house, she was made aware that it was less than ten minutes from the hospital. But then in a town the size of Armidale most homes were only that distance from where the hospital was located.

As she stepped outside into the cold morning she couldn't help but notice the scent of the country air envelop her. It stopped her in her tracks for the briefest moment. The perfume from the large eucalyptus tree in the neighbouring yard travelled on the chilly breeze. There was no smog, no smell of heavy early morning traffic or industry. The fresh, naturally scented air was one of life's simple pleasures that she hadn't realised she had been missing.

Until that moment.

She wondered if there was anything else that this country town might remind her that she had been missing. A year of relatively short-term placements arranged by a national medical locum agency was beginning to grow old for Jessica, but she was scared to stop. Scared to consider other options. A sense of safety came from having the decision of what to do next made by a third party. And the security that came from not forming relationships, other than with colleagues, sat well with Jessica. While there was a sense of emptiness that couldn't be ignored, she decided that was better than the pain of heartache that came from getting close and having it fall apart.

Moments later as she drove along, with a little nervousness stirring in her stomach as it tended to on the first day in a new role, she tried to avoid looking down at her clothes. She cringed as she caught sight of her jeans, sweater and grey and lime-green runners and prayed her bags would arrive from Sydney that morning as promised.

'I'm Errol Langridge. It's so lovely to meet you, Dr Ayers, and, speaking on behalf of the Board of the Armidale Regional Memorial Hospital, we're thrilled to have you on staff, albeit for a short time.' The older, impeccably dressed man shook Jessica's hand gently but for the longest time. His clothing had a country feel in the blue and white check shirt and chambray trousers but the quality of both was evident. And the sincerity of his words shone through the smile in his pale blue eyes. 'Quite a coup for us, if I do say so myself. Not often that we have a temporary position filled by someone as experienced as yourself.

Short contracts are usually taken up by those straight out of medical school.'

'I'm very happy to be here, Professor Langridge,' Jessica replied, well aware of the status of the older doctor. She had noted his title on the letter he had sent to her when she'd accepted the role. 'And please, Jessica is fine by me.'

'And you must use Errol. Equality for both sexes, plus it makes me feel less than my sixty-eight years if you use my first name.'

'Then Errol it is.'

The Professor smiled a half smile before his expression became serious with the sudden sound of an impending ambulance. The main doors of the hospital opened just as the vehicle pulled into the bay and the sound carried into the foyer. He motioned for Jessica to follow him down the corridor. His steps were fast and purposeful as he turned his head slightly to speak over his shoulder to her.

'I think now is as good a time as any to visit the ER. You'll see our staff doing what they do best. And, once the commotion subsides, I'll introduce you to our Head of ER, Harrison Wainwright. You'll be working closely with him, no doubt, as many of our paediatric patients are admitted from there. He's been at the hospital for so long he's almost an institution, although he's still the good side of forty, unlike most of us in senior roles. He's a tough taskmaster but it works for most; besides, we can't seem to get rid of him anyway.'

Jessica's eyes widened and her mouth drew tight as she quickly caught up with the older man. She hoped it would work for her too. Working alongside a man with an attitude was not on her wish list, particularly one they couldn't get rid of, perhaps due to his connections or watertight contract. She suddenly felt her stomach churn again. Paediatrics was a long way from ER and hopefully their paths would not cross too often during the six weeks.

Without taking a breath, the Professor continued as his eyes wrinkled in laughter, 'You must forgive my sense of humour or, as my wife says, my bad taste in jokes. We are eternally grateful that he's never indicated he wants to leave us. He actually grew up around this part of the world and we're glad he returned. The hospital couldn't function without him. He's brilliant and I can't praise him enough and the medical students and patients love him. The nurses do too, but for very different reasons, I'm sure.'

Jessica wasn't quite sure how to take the Professor's conflicting character reference for her colleague as she followed him into the Emergency Department. While he'd quelled her concerns on one hand, she certainly didn't want to go near the reason the nurses loved the man.

A stretcher suddenly rushed past them, making Jessica draw in her breath as if that would give them more room. It was a silly reaction and made no sense to her, particularly as a doctor accustomed to the Emergency Department of a great number of hospitals, but not much had made sense in the last few days. The first patient, a young woman, had been immobilised with a cervical collar, so a neck injury had clearly been suspected by the paramedics, and her right leg was in a splint; by her appearance, Jessica assumed she was a teenager. She stepped back again quickly as a second barouche approached them.

'Motor vehicle accident,' the paramedic began as they wheeled the patients into bays opposite each other as directed by the nursing staff. 'Two passengers. Female suspected spinal cord injury, broken ankle and minor lacerations. Male with lacerations to hand and forehead. No other visible or apparent injury.'

The second accompanying young male patient had a bandage to his head but he was alert and firing questions at everyone. His hand was also bandaged but other than that he appeared unscathed by whatever incident had occurred. A female paramedic attempted to calm and comfort him but it appeared to be to no avail. Quickly the medical team approached and an immediate handover ensued. The second patient was assigned two nurses and a young doctor, whom she suspected was an intern, while the first with the serious injuries had the attention of many more of the ER staff. The alert patient was distressed but appeared under control.

Suddenly another stretcher entered the ER

with two paramedics in tow. 'Hit and run on Mundy Street. Suspected fractured femur. Female, seventy-three years of age.'

'Dr Steele, once you assess your patient, if there's no immediate risk, please leave him with the nurses and attend to our elderly patient,' a deep voice called out from beside the young female patient in the adjacent bay. Jessica could see the back of a tall man in a white consultant's coat. He stood over six foot, close to six foot two, she guessed. The deepest brown, almost black hair and a commanding presence by the way everyone looked to him for instruction. She suspected he was the Head of ER about whom Errol had been speaking only moments earlier.

Jessica watched the young doctor speak briefly with the two nurses and then, as instructed, head over to the paramedics and the new arrival.

It certainly was a busy Emergency Department, just as Errol had told her only minutes before, but it was running smoothly and that was no easy task as there were already patients in another two bays being attended by staff.

Jessica couldn't help but agree the department was a well-oiled machine. No one hesitated or appeared to be second-guessing. The Head of ER was, in Jessica's mind, to be admired. It took a high level of calm, an ability to triage patients and manage staff with a good understanding of their strengths and their skills to maintain a calm environment for the patients.

Jessica watched on in silence as the empty bay was filled with another patient, transferred from the stretcher onto the hospital gurney. That level of synergy and professionalism was exactly what she hoped to maintain in Paediatrics during her time at the hospital.

But within moments that very calm began to dissipate.

The young man left in the nurses' care suddenly tugged his arm away from the petite nurse and attempted to climb down from the bed. His feet were almost on the ground.

'It's all my fault…it's all my fault,' he repeated loudly, the words spurred by unbridled emotion. 'I need to see her. I need to say sorry and see she's okay.'

Jessica was aware the young nurse was

struggling to contain the situation and the ER did not need an overly emotional patient breaking free and interfering with another patient's treatment in order to purge his guilt.

Jessica spun around to the dispenser behind her and donned a pair of disposable gloves and a disposable gown from the top of a nearby pile. 'Excuse me, Professor. I'd like to start my shift now, if that's all right with you.'

Errol looked a little confused but nodded as Jessica headed over to the bay where the ruckus was taking place.

'I'm Dr Ayers and I'd like to help you,' she announced as she firmly placed her hand on his legs and then lifted them back onto the gurney.

The nurses both looked at Jessica in surprise and she picked up on their confusion.

'I thought you could use some assistance. I'm locum Paediatric Consultant. I commenced at the hospital this morning and must apologise that I've not been issued with my ID yet,' she told them as she motioned towards Errol, aware her current clothing, still visible under the thin blue gown, made her look anything but a medical professional. 'Professor Langridge can vouch for me.'

The older nurse glanced over at Errol, who was nodding his consent, while the younger one took Jessica at face value and together they attempted to control the situation.

'Can you please give me your name?' Jessica asked the young patient while she assessed the proximity of the medical equipment within the bay. A stethoscope lay on the portable trolley nearby so she scooped it up and popped it around her neck. The young man began to calm slightly as if he knew fighting was futile as the nurse attached the monitors to him to record his heart rate, blood pressure and oxygen saturation.

'I want to help you while the medical team in the bay opposite help the young woman who came in with you. Her injuries clearly appear more serious but we will be undertaking a medical examination of you to ensure that yours are in fact only superficial. In motor vehicle accidents you can sustain internal injuries that are not instantly apparent. Before I begin, can I have please have your full name and age?'

'Cody Smith, and that's my girlfriend over there,' he said as he raised his hand and pointed to the other bay.

'Can you please give me her name and age?' the young nurse asked. 'So I can pass that information onto the ER team looking after her.'

'Let me tell them,' he said, trying to pull away from the nurses again. 'I just want to say I'm sorry to her.'

'That won't be happening. Please remain still; I need to check your eyes.' Jessica's words were firm and to the point as she held his chin and shone the light into the young man's left eye and then the right one.

'My eyes are fine. They're not bleedin' or nothing.'

'Cody, as I said before, some injuries are not obvious so there won't necessarily be bleeding, but a mild head injury can still be sustained from a car accident. You may have suffered whiplash and it can result in impaired vision or other problems and symptoms are varied. Do you have trouble focusing your eyes when switching your gaze between near and far objects?'

'Nah, I'm good,' he replied. 'I can read the exit sign and her name thing.' He pointed to the nurse's identification tag.

'Do you feel nauseous, as if you are going to vomit when you look around?'

'Nah, I'm all good, I told you already. It's me girlfriend I'm worried about.'

'No, Cody. That is not an option,' she continued. 'Even if you are fine, you need to understand that if you were to rush over there to help her, you would in fact be doing just the opposite. You could get in the way of the medical team and put your girlfriend at risk.'

'I don't wanna do nothing but help her.'

'Then, as the nurse said, you can help her by giving us her name and age.'

'Ginny Randolf. She's seventeen.'

'Thank you,' Jessica said as she continued the examination and noted his response to the light stimulation was within normal limits.

'I'll pass on her details and come right back,' the younger nurse said as she headed over to the other patient.

'And how old are you?' Jessica enquired while checking the young man's pupils for dilation.

'I'm sixteen.'

'Okay, Cody, we are going to have to take some blood samples and check your alcohol level. Have you been drinking?'

'No. I'm on my probationary licence. That's not why we crashed. Is that what you think happened? Do you think I was drink-driving?' His voice was shrill and once again Jessica needed to placate him.

'I'm not assuming anything.' Her voice was low and calm as she met his eyes. 'This is routine and *not* because I suspect anything, Cody. It's just that with any motor vehicle accident a blood test for alcohol and other drugs is mandatory.'

'I can't drink on a probationary licence. I'm an apprentice chippy. I'm not looking to lose my job with a baby on the way. Ginny's nine weeks pregnant.'

Jessica and the nurse immediately looked at each other and, without a word exchanged, the second nurse disappeared to pass on the crucial information. Pregnancy would certainly complicate the situation if there were suspected internal injuries and the chance of miscarriage was a concern.

'We found out a few weeks ago.'

He rested back down on his elbows, not taking his eyes off the opposite bay but seemingly finally accepting the need to comply—and the fact a towering male nurse had just approached to assist would not allow him to do otherwise.

'We were arguing about when she would tell her parents. They don't like me. I wanted her to hold off a bit longer so they didn't try to force her to get rid of the baby. She told me she was gonna tell them tonight and I got scared and distracted and I didn't see the merging lane. We went off the road and hit the fence.'

A nurse suddenly pulled a curtain around the young man's girlfriend.

'What's happening? Why are they doing that? Is she okay?' Cody's questions came flying at Jessica and the nurse as he sat bolt upright again.

'Your girlfriend is in good hands,' Jessica

told him. 'And, thanks to you, the team know there's another tiny life growing inside of her so they will be doing everything possible to treat them both.'

'Please can you go and check? I need to know what's happening. I'm freaking out here. She's gotta be okay.'

Jessica reluctantly agreed. She wasn't even officially on staff yet so not keen to overstep protocols further than she already had but she knew Cody's anxious state was escalating by the minute with the curtain obscuring his view and it wouldn't end well if he raced over there. The young man was physically fine and the other nurses had returned to monitor his observations so she headed over to enquire about the status of his partner—the mother of his unborn child.

With each step she took, she prayed fate would not change the course of their young lives.

She quietly and tentatively parted the curtain and peered inside the bay to see the back of the doctor undertaking an ultrasound examination of the young woman. He had been informed of her pregnancy and was obviously prioritising the baby. It all seemed calm so she didn't feel the need to interrupt.

'The baby is fine; there's a strong heartbeat and no obvious signs of distress, Ginny,' she heard him say. 'I'm sorry you can't see the screen that I am looking at right now. I can share those images later with you. But for the time being we need to keep you flat until we can properly assess the damage to your neck and back. I believe it is muscular as you do not have any of the symptoms I would expect to see with a spinal injury. I need to send you for an MRI—it's not an X-ray so it's perfectly safe for your baby and it will allow us to assess any neck, spinal or ankle injuries. You and your baby are both paramount to anything we do.'

Jessica agreed with his treatment plan and she thought he had a lovely bedside manner and comforting voice. Deep, masculine but still warm. It sounded familiar but she knew that couldn't be the case. She didn't know anyone in town.

She raised her hand to close the curtain and caught sight of his profile and all but gasped.

Her heart took a leap as she recognised him. She did know him. But the last time she'd seen him he wasn't wearing a white consultant's coat. Instead he was wearing the wet imprint of her carry-on luggage on his shoe.

CHAPTER THREE

JESSICA WAS MOMENTARILY SPEECHLESS.

Harrison Wainwright had been on the plane with her, so was he the doctor she had been told had just flown in on the long-haul flight from LA with the romance writers? She imagined the odds were weighted in favour of him being the one, particularly in a country city of this size. But, wherever he had flown in from, he was the one she had managed to run over. The one who'd captured her attention and piqued her curiosity. And the one she had not been able to erase from her mind.

As she closed the curtain there was a stirring in the pit of her stomach. But this stirring was not nerves. It was as if she had been reunited with someone she knew. There was a familiarity with the man that was inexplicable. As if they had a connection. Not from the incident at the airport; it was something more. Something they had once shared…or were about to share. Something that had kept her awake the previous night, thinking about him. But they hadn't shared anything more than a fleeting uncomfortable meeting and they wouldn't share anything more than that, she reminded herself. She didn't know the man, let alone have a connection. Nor did she want one with Dr Harrison Wainwright or any man.

Of that fact Jessica was resolute, but she was also scared and confused by her reaction. She hadn't been able to forget him since their chance meeting the day before and that was something she was trying to ignore. She wished his face hadn't been etched on her mind but she suddenly realised it had subconsciously, or not so subconsciously, been there for almost twenty-four hours.

Taking a deep breath, she tried to exhale feelings that were beginning to stir with him so near to her again. She hadn't felt anything close to what she was feeling at that moment in longer than she could remember and that was by design. She had controlled her emotions, kept them in check without too much effort. It had been safe for her to be around men of her age, or even ten years either side, because she felt nothing but indifference. She didn't trust them in the slightest. In her mind, few had anything other than a desire to get what they wanted at any cost.

Tom had destroyed her trust in men, and love, and the whole damned thing and she was angry. Angry because Tom had taken her innocent view of the world and twisted it into a level of bitterness she had never wanted or expected to ever feel. Never imagined she could feel. He had robbed her of her belief in happily ever after. She wished it wasn't the case but nothing and no one had or would be able to give her reason to change her outlook. Jessica was starting to believe the moulds were broken after her father's generation of men. Those men had treated women with respect and love. And commitment had meant something. But the new generation of men were shallow and insincere and she felt sorry for women who fell in love. She would never do so again.

* * *

Jessica was relieved that Harrison hadn't seen her as he was too distracted with his patient but she quickly realised that she could not avoid the inevitable. Professor Langridge was about to introduce them so she had no choice but to meet him. She couldn't avoid it. They would be working together. To what extent she wasn't sure, but there would be mutual patients during the course of her short tenure.

Her forehead wrinkled slightly with concern at the thought and her heart began to race a little faster than usual. And it had nothing to do with embarrassment over the silly incident. She wasn't sure if he would even remember that. It was more how her body was reacting to being near him. And the feelings were bringing a warmth to her body. Almost a dizzy rush. It was not like her. She hadn't experienced so many conflicting emotions in such a short space of time. Ever. Pre, post or even during her time with the man she'd thought she was going to marry.

The new mysterious man had been consuming her thoughts for no good reason. And with that came an overwhelming concern about her appearance. Her clothes were completely unsuitable for ER. Why had she not travelled in something nicer? Ordinarily Jessica would have prioritised her wardrobe and asked the cab driver to wait, but that morning she had been running a little late and was anxious he might drive off, causing her to miss her flight. She hadn't wanted to risk it, so she'd raced out of the door in an outfit more befitting walking a trail.

It was out of character for the old Jessica, who always made sure that she was well groomed and elegantly dressed. Even if her skirt and blouse were hidden by a consulting coat. At least she knew she was wearing something smart, and her shoes and earrings were in plain sight even if they were very conservative. Some days Jessica would look in the mirror and think that perhaps her clothing was more befitting someone twenty or thirty years older, but it suited the new her. The Jessica who avoided anything overtly feminine. Since discovering she had unwittingly become someone's mistress she had spent many sleepless nights wondering if she had attracted her lover by the way she dressed. Her choice in clothing had never been overly revealing but she couldn't help but question whether he would have looked twice if she had chosen a different look. Perhaps that had nothing to do with it, perhaps it did, but her new wardrobe sent a clear message to everyone.

She was not interested in anything other than being the best doctor she could be and even thinking about a man did not factor into her day.

Until that moment when she'd felt very self-conscious and almost like a giddy teenager, unable to control her emotions. She was so confused. It was so out of character with the reinvented Jessica of late. Perhaps, she thought, it was because she was tired and that made her anxious and unsettled. Not that the bed hadn't been comfortable the night before; it was and she had slept well, all things considered.

No, Jessica's version of tired was different. She was tired of running. Tired of new beginnings that never changed how she felt about herself. And so tired of the unrelenting late-night thoughts of how she should have done things differently. How she could have managed everything better. But she hadn't and she was living with the consequences. Trying to find peace and forget her time as *the other woman*. Focus on her career and forget about love. There was no room for it in her life or her heart. She was all about work. Her sole focus was to live her life as a single professional woman, respected for her work ethic.

But the next step in her professional journey had been thwarted by delayed luggage. Professionalism had flown out of the window and soccer mum had flown in and there was not a damned thing she could do about it.

She made her way back to check on Cody and reassure him that the baby and his partner were both fine.

'Ginny is being taken for an MRI—'

'What's that? Will it hurt her or the baby?'

'MRI is an abbreviation of magnetic resonance imaging. It's a safe alternative to an X-ray and presents no danger to the baby during the first trimester, which is the first twelve weeks of the pregnancy.'

'Why's she having it?'

'The doctor wants to check that Ginny hasn't sustained any neck or spinal injuries as a result of the accident. He can also check the damage to her ankle.'

Just then another doctor appeared and introduced himself. 'I'm John Steele, the ER Resident.'

'Hi, I'm Jessica Ayers, the Paediatric locum.'

'I know—the nurses filled me in,' he replied with a smile that showed he had orthodontic braces in place. 'Welcome aboard and thanks for stepping in. I heard it's your first day and you're already part of the team.'

'Happy to help.'

'You're going to fit right in; we can all tell,' he told her and then picked up Cody's notes. 'The nurses think you're awesome already and they're a pretty tough lot to impress. So, you're off to a flying start if you can manage that in the first five minutes. Have you met Dr Wainwright yet? He's our ER Consultant.'

Jessica shook her head and swallowed. She didn't know what to say. While she hadn't been formally introduced, she had met him in an unconventional way.

'Anyway, we've held you up long enough. I can take over here if you want to head up to Paediatrics?'

'Okay. Great…and it's lovely to meet you, John.'

'Likewise.'

Jessica turned back to find the Professor still waiting for her. He had a warm expression on his face. Ordinarily that, combined with John Steele's welcoming demeanour, would have put her at ease but Jessica felt anything but relaxed. She wished she had gone straight to Paediatrics and not stopped in the ER and she could have delayed the awkward meeting that she knew was about to take place unless there was another rush of patients through the Emergency Room doors. And by the lack of sirens it was clear that wasn't about to happen.

As Jessica pulled free her gown and gloves and dropped them in the bin, she watched Harrison Wainwright walking towards them. She knew she had to simply accept the situation and move on, as she had been doing for the best part of a year.

'Errol, what brings you to the ER?' Harrison asked.

'This young lady, actually,' the Professor replied. 'May I introduce you to...'

'Jessica Ayers—Dr Jessica Ayers.' Jessica couldn't believe that her nerves had caused her to interrupt a professional introduction and repeat her name, adding her title. So now she was both rude and badly dressed. She was mortified by her behaviour and dying a little inside by her own actions. What had happened to the cool medical professional who'd just stepped into the ER and helped out without making a fool of herself? Where was she now? What was going on in her head to make her behave so strangely? She knew the answer. He was standing right in front of her.

The Professor shot a quizzical smile in Jessica's direction, coughed to clear his throat and continued. 'Dr Ayers is our new Paediatric Consultant and very *enthusiastic* to meet everyone, it would appear.'

Jessica wanted to jump into a non-existent hole in the linoleum floor of the ER but there was no such hole, no saviour of the awkward beyond belief moment, so she did what she had been doing for the past twelve months—she saved herself. She drew in a deep breath and extended her hand to Harrison. He met her handshake but she couldn't help but notice that his eyes left hers momentarily and travelled to her feet. She was under no illusion as to what he was thinking, more than likely silently questioning why she had fronted up on her first day dressed as if she was going on a hike. She braced herself for the mention of her inappropriate attire. While Errol had not mentioned it, she felt sure that someone, perhaps Harrison, would say something.

'Welcome aboard, Dr Ayers,' he replied. 'However, this isn't the first time we've met.'

Jessica stiffened. Of course he would remember that the *enthusiastic* locum had also run over his foot the day before. Terrible first impression followed by an unprofessional second impression. She could hardly wait to see how she could trump either. Throwing up from nerves and embarrassment was a possible contender.

'So, you know each other?' Errol asked with his eyes widening.

'No,' Jessica quickly announced.

'Yes,' came Harrison's response only seconds later.

'Well, which is it?' the Professor asked with a quizzical frown. 'Yes or no?'

'Well, we technically don't *know* each other,' Jessica responded.

'We bumped into each other at the airport yesterday. Quite literally,' Harrison explained.

Errol's glance darted back to Jessica for confirmation.

Jessica cringed and nodded in his direction. 'I ran over him.' Then, turning her attention back to Harrison, she continued, 'I'm so sorry. I'm not usually that clumsy.'

'It happens,' he told her with an almost impish smile she didn't want to see in his eyes.

'Well, I must say you're a good sport, Harrison,' Errol stated. 'And clearly you weren't travelling too fast, Jessica, because there's no visible injuries. Were you on a scooter?'

'No, I didn't run *him* over… I *ran over* him… with a suitcase.'

'And there's not a scratch to show for it,' Harrison added.

Jessica felt her skin prickle—his voice was as deep, husky and reassuring as it had been the day before.

'I'm confused so I think I'll leave it there,' Errol said with a frown creasing his brow yet again.

'It wasn't hard to do, particularly in a bustling international airport like Armidale,' Harrison continued, adding a cheeky grin that threw her emotions into free fall.

She didn't say anything. She wanted to pull her eyes away but she couldn't. She stood frozen. Her head and heart were in turmoil. She felt certain she had experienced almost all possible emotions in the previous five minutes.

'Again, I'm still terribly confused and I have a Board meeting in fifteen minutes. I'm going to leave you to get acquainted, or *reacquainted*, whichever the case may be.' With that, Errol stepped away but not before adding, 'Welcome again, Jessica, to the Armidale

Regional Memorial. I'm very glad to have you on board. I have a very good feeling about this.'

Jessica feigned a smile as all the while she was thinking just the opposite. There was nothing good about any of it. In fact, she had a very bad feeling. And it had nothing to do with the hospital or Errol. It had everything to do with the man standing before her.

'So, you're our newbie to the hospital then, Dr Ayers?' Harrison asked, leaning in a bit closer.

'Yes, and please call me Jessica,' she insisted then couldn't think of anything to add. She could and would normally drive the conversation but suddenly she was searching for something to say. Her mind was befuddled by thoughts that had no place being there. And senses were coming into play that had been dormant for a long time. His cologne was subtle to the level of being almost impossible to detect by anyone else with the overpowering scent of sanitising products used in the ER but, unfortunately for Jessica, it was not lost on her. His body warmth was bringing out the masculine notes of sandalwood and she could feel the beat of her own pulse reacting.

'If it makes you feel better, my shoes dried without a mark. Nothing to indicate that I'd been steamrolled by your runaway luggage.'

Harrison smiled a wide smile that lit up his chiselled face. It made him look even more handsome, but Jessica couldn't help but notice that while it was a genuine smile it seemed slightly guarded. She'd thought she was the only one who walked around at war with herself and the world. Then again, perhaps she was imagining something defensive that wasn't there. After all, they were in the ER so his mind would be on the job of managing the rapid response unit of the largest hospital in the New England region.

At that moment she didn't trust her instincts. And that made her uneasy. In fact, everything about her current situation and, more to the point, Dr Harrison Wainwright made her uneasy. She cursed under her breath. Why couldn't her colleague be the same age as Errol? It would have been far more convenient for her because a handsome and now slightly

intriguing man who appeared pleasantly surprised that they would be working together
was the last thing she needed. Now or ever.

Harrison was surprised by the level of happiness he was experiencing on seeing the mysterious blonde traveller again. And to learn
that they would be working together. It should
have worried him, but it didn't. Strangely, he
felt elated by the idea. He had fallen asleep
thinking about her. Wondering if and when
he might see her again. She was clearly gorgeous, but there were a lot of gorgeous women
in New England and he had casually dated a
few over the years. But his attraction to the
stranger in town was more than skin-deep.
He was intrigued by her. He had no clue why,
after such a brief encounter, but it was undeniable.

Not for a moment had he imagined they
would be working together. He had so many
questions. Her reason for coming to Armidale for one. Skilled enough to impress the
Board of the hospital—that meant she would

certainly be in demand in other hospitals. So why choose here? he wondered.

He glanced at her hand and then lifted his eyes just as quickly, but not before he noticed there was no ring indicating a husband or fiancé, but that didn't mean she was single. Why did he care? He had no clue but he was pleasantly surprised to see the absence of jewellery on her hand. Harrison wanted to kick himself for having any interest in the paediatrician's relationship status. For five years he hadn't cared about anyone's relationship status; he had been too preoccupied trying to sort out his own. Although he'd known his marriage was just a piece of paper—any love or commitment he felt was solely focused on his child—still, he had taken a long time to officially end it. His wife's decision to walk away from both him and their child had painfully but effectively ended any feelings he'd had for her many years before.

Dr Jessica Ayers was stirring more than curiosity and Harrison was at odds with how he felt and how he believed he should be feeling. They were poles apart.

* * *

At that moment the doors to the ER burst open again and two paramedics with a single stretcher rushed in.

'Male, unidentified, suspected methamphetamine overdose,' the taller of the paramedics announced as he steered the barouche past the nurses' station while the other held a cold compress on the young man's head and kept in place another pack that was resting across his chest. Intravenous fluids were being administered and Jessica could see he had been restrained.

'Bay three,' the senior nurse, whom Jessica was yet to meet, announced as she crossed to meet them, signalling for the nurse she had already met while treating Cody and a young woman to follow her. By the third woman's very young and very nervous appearance and the fact that the Armidale Regional Memorial Hospital was a teaching facility, Jessica assumed she was a medical student. Quickly her suspicions were confirmed when the nurse continued, 'Melissa, ask any questions you like; don't be shy. Your first student placement can seem daunting but we're here to help.'

'You have to love the rush of a Monday morning,' Harrison muttered to Jessica before stepping away and crossing to the allocated bay. He donned sterile gloves while the paramedics transferred the patient to the hospital bed and replaced the restraints. 'Fill me in.' His voice was serious and his words short.

'The young man was found slumped by a dumpster just off Beardy Street by one of the store owners ten minutes ago. No ID and he's not known to us, so either not a regular user or new to town, as we know our regulars. It's an area frequented by the methamphetamine crowd after hours. He appeared unconscious initially; however, when we attempted to engage it became obvious he was crashing from some illegal substance. He was suffering from hallucinations and kept referring to ants eating him alive and this presumably initiated the repetitive motor activity in his legs. It then escalated to verbal abuse towards us before he collapsed with chest pain and shortness of breath. He calmed down so I'd say we found him at the end of the crash. Within two minutes of getting him on board his irregular heartbeat came close to normal.'

'Do we have any clues on the amount taken; if it was snorted or smoked; and any idea on how long ago the drug was consumed?'

'Negative to all three. If he had any mates, they took off. If anyone witnessed him crashing they didn't stay to help or fill us in on the details.'

'Why doesn't that surprise me?' Harrison said, shaking his head in frustration. 'Vitals?'

'We recorded an initial elevated body temperature of thirty-nine point five but managed to bring it down slightly with cold compresses. His BPM was also raised but that's stabilised now.'

'Great work, guys,' Harrison replied then turned to the senior nurse. 'Alison, start gastric lavage and administer activated charcoal.'

Harrison continued issuing instructions as he began an examination of the clearly agitated but still restrained patient. He lifted the oxygen mask and carefully inspected the patient's mouth before replacing the apparatus.

'His dentation appears reasonable, as does his weight, which would indicate an acute overdose and a fairly recent entree to meth. Let's hope with counselling we can redirect his path before he heads into chronic misuse and the myriad of psychological and medical issues that would arise over time.'

The younger nurse hooked the IV already in place to a stand and cleared the paramedics to leave. 'Thanks, guys, for bringing him in. And Brian, say hi to Mum for me and see you next weekend.'

Jessica was close enough to hear everything and she was quickly reminded by the level of familiarity between the nurse and paramedic that she was in a country hospital where everyone knew each other on some level.

'Sure will, Phoebe, Tommo's birthday bash should be awesome,' the younger paramedic replied as they exited the ER, but not before stopping at the nurses' station to sign off on the paperwork.

'I want full bloods, an ECG and a urine sample. By the look and smell of this poor boy he's lost control of his bladder and he's wearing his last sample,' Harrison continued. 'He'll pull through but his long-term prognosis isn't good if he doesn't clean up his act. Can you call up and see if there are any beds available? I'd like to admit him and give him time to see a counsellor either today or tomorrow before we let him back on the streets.'

Jessica could see the unkempt young man's trousers were stained and the foul stench coming from his direction made it clear he had either no awareness of self-care or no means by which to maintain any level of hygiene.

'I'll check. We're not at capacity at the moment, so we might be able to keep him overnight,' Alison replied. 'We'll get him into a hospital gown and reach out for some new clothes from the Salvation Army; they're always happy to send in something clean for cases like this.' She swabbed his arm before taking a sample for the blood work; all the while the now compliant patient lay still, albeit for his restless legs that randomly moved away from his imaginary foe.

Harrison stepped away, as did the medical student. As they left the bay, Harrison reached up and closed the blue curtains. Then he turned his attention to the young woman still hovering awkwardly nearby, apparently unsure of what to do next. 'Melissa, now we have the young man stable, what can you tell me about your textbook and hands-on experience with methamphetamine abuse?'

Jessica watched as Melissa shifted a little on her feet.

'Um…nothing first-hand as this is my first hospital placement. But I know the psychosis resulting from a chronic methamphetamine overdose can last up to twelve months sometimes, with permanent effects of paranoia and ongoing memory loss. Meth abuse by the patient can also result in delusions, repeated infections, rotted teeth, weight loss, skin sores, and they can even suffer a stroke or heart attack, no matter their age.'

'That's correct. Recovery from a methamphetamine overdose depends on the amount of drug that was taken, how long it was abused, and how quickly treatment for the methamphetamine overdose symptoms was administered. The earlier a patient gets medical assistance for a methamphetamine overdose, the better the outcome. Anything else you can add?'

'Methamphetamine is classified as a Schedule II stimulant drug, and it works by affecting the central nervous symptom. It's similar in structure to amphetamine but far stronger and also more addictive. Legally it's only available through a prescription and generally prescribed to treat narcolepsy.'

'I'm impressed, Melissa. Is this an area of interest for you?' Harrison commented as he took the clipboard from the senior nurse, who had just approached him to authorise both the tests and the patient's admittance into the hospital. The nurse then left with the signed documents.

'My father's a pharmacist in Tamworth so he always lectured us about drugs and the potential for them to be abused. We saw a lot of it on the streets there when I was growing up. It's everywhere, like a pandemic in the cities and the regions now.'

'Unfortunately, you're right and let's hope

this young man stops before he heads down the road of chronic abuse.'

'His chances are, unfortunately, going to be slim at best,' Jessica stated. 'Unless he can extract himself from his current situation and, depending on the depth of his addiction, enter a rehabilitation programme. There needs to be a holistic approach to turning the young person's life around. Without changing the situation, one night in hospital is a band-aid that will, unfortunately, fall off very quickly in the real world.'

Jessica's response was born of experience and she considered Harrison's decision to admit him overnight was textbook optimistic but not practical. She was no longer a bright-eyed, bushy-tailed medical student who thought following procedure ensured a good outcome. At times like this she felt battle-worn. She had seen it all, and couldn't erase the vision of the tiny skeletal frame of one of her patients, nor the wounds on another twelve-year-old's once pretty face, self-inflicted during a bout of hallucinations. She had cried herself to sleep over the injustice and wished she could wrap every child in the warmth of her arms and protect them. But she couldn't. Her professional innocence had been stolen bit by bit as she'd witnessed the children ravaged by drugs and the parents who couldn't help because they had been using themselves.

On all fronts Jessica was a long way from the young medical student standing before her. She acknowledged for a fleeting moment that she had been just like that young woman once, and there were days when she wished she could be again. Wide-eyed and hopeful for the future. But not any more.

Harrison paused to study Jessica. His look was pensive. He said nothing for a moment but she could see he was surprised by her matter-of-fact honesty. Jessica worried it might have been too blunt but she had reason to be harsh when it came to seeing children in her paediatric ward suffering from drug abuse. She felt so sad and helpless at times.

'I couldn't agree more,' Harrison told her, interrupting her thoughts and echoing her feelings. 'Bloody frustrating and such a waste. And I'm fully aware that one night won't do anything more than keep him off the street and stop him OD-ing in the next eight hours. It won't turn his life around, Jessica, but what it will do is buy us some time to schedule an appointment with a counsellor and a social worker, who might be able to make a difference. We heal the bodies and hope our colleagues can begin the process of healing their minds and broken spirits and, with a good deal of luck, lead them away from the destructive path they're on right now.'

Jessica was taken aback by his response. It was honest but heartfelt and far from textbook and naïve. Clearly, he was as frustrated as her and trying his best with the resources he had. Harrison was a realist with a heart.

Harrison turned his attention back to Melissa and the task at hand—educating the next generation of doctors.

'Do you know what they call methamphetamine on the street?' Harrison questioned Melissa.

'Ice?' Melissa asked.

'Yes, and there are other terms their friends

may use when they drop them off at the Emergency Department,' he continued.

'I've not heard it referred to by any other name.'

'Speed,' Jessica cut in as she stepped closer. 'Or crank, tweak, Christina, Tina, chalk… Oh, and *go fast*. That's the latest. I think I've heard them all.'

'Well, that's quite a comprehensive list. You've got the street lingo down pat,' Harrison replied with a curious expression on his face. 'You're clearly passionate about the topic but I didn't think you'd see much of it in Paediatrics. I was under the impression that yours was a slightly more protected unit from the effects of drug abuse, at least by the age of your patients. I've not seen any under seventeen present here.'

'How I wish I didn't know quite so much but I've seen it with a regularity that I despise and one that scares me, particularly in the major cities. Some as young as eleven years of age present suffering from drug abuse in Paediatrics.'

'Eleven?' Melissa's voice rose in shock at Jessica's statement.

'Yes, only two months ago I was consulting in a public hospital in Melbourne and a little girl presented suffering the effects of methamphetamine. She was two weeks shy of her twelfth birthday.'

'What about her parents? Where were they?'

'Doing the same, unfortunately. Chronic users.'

'So her environment was stacked against her,' Melissa said flatly.

'In this case, yes, but not always.'

'If only there was some sort of prerequisite or testing to being a parent. It's hard to break the cycle if a child grows up with it,' Melissa commented as she rolled her eyes.

'Yes, parenting is a huge responsibility and a tough role at times, no doubt, but in my book if you sign on to have a child, then you sign on for life,' Jessica said with conviction. 'Once you're a parent, then I think your own needs have to come second to theirs, but maybe that's an old-fashioned view. And who am I to say, since I don't have any children of my own? I'm sure in this day and age it's not easy raising them and with so many parents doing it alone it must be a struggle at times.'

Harrison said nothing for a moment. Jessica felt his gaze upon her. It lingered and it made her feel very self-conscious but it didn't feel as if he was judging her. Quite the opposite; it was a look of something that felt like pride. Which was crazy because he didn't know her and she worried from her harsh comments that she might be perceived by him as borderline jaded.

He suddenly averted his gaze and turned to Melissa. 'I hope you get a good block of rotation time in our Paediatric Unit with Dr Ayers. I think she'll be invaluable in your journey. She's certainly opened my eyes to many things this morning. There were definitely a few things I didn't expect to hear.'

CHAPTER FOUR

'HAVE YOU UNDERTAKEN the hospital induction or did the Professor just bring you straight to the ER?' Harrison asked, interrupting Jessica's thoughts and his own.

And his own thoughts needed interrupting. They had been filling his mind for longer than just the short time since he and Jessica had been formally introduced. Once again, he silently admitted that he had given the gorgeous doctor more space in his head than he'd planned after their airport encounter and he had hoped their paths would cross again. Maybe at the grocery store or a restaurant. He'd pictured potential scenarios and wondered if she would run over his foot with a shopping trolley...or sit at a table adjacent to his and drop a fork on his shoe. His thoughts did not shift from recalling her beautiful, slightly embarrassed smile when they'd first met and he'd caught himself smiling too. For the first time in a very long time.

He also remembered the sense of relief that had washed over him as he'd alighted the plane, realising that the custody battle was over. His son would never be at risk of being taken from him again. Bryce was too young to understand that the two of them ever being parted had been a threat, but it had consumed Harrison for most of his son's life. Not knowing if or when his son could be taken for months, or longer, to the other side of the world, to a woman his son couldn't remember, but one he would need to acknowledge as his mother.

But those worries were gone. Now all Harrison had to do was lodge the divorce papers once they were sent over from the attorney in the US. He had done his part; now his soon-to-be ex-wife just had to do the same. He knew there wouldn't be a problem, as she had a new partner and wanted to move on, which was why she had agreed to give him full custody. It was almost a cliché. The new man in her life was considerably older, very wealthy, well connected in the film industry and he didn't want anything to do with children.

Last night, as he'd thrown another log onto the open fire, having tucked his son into bed, Harrison had leant on the fireplace staring into flames that danced and leapt and finally enveloped the new wood. He had sipped on his gin and tonic as the wood snapped and split along a jagged crevice, releasing steam and filling the softly lit room with a warm glow and a burst of heat. And he'd felt a glimmer of hope. It wasn't relief; it was more than that. He wasn't sure what he was hopeful of but he knew he felt that he had left his worries behind. And, unexpectedly, he also had something to look forward to and that was just the chance that he might see the mystery woman again. It didn't make any sense to him, but he couldn't pretend his mood hadn't changed in the last twenty-four hours. It had. And he believed there were two reasons.

Perhaps the second had been born of the first. Finally, he could let down his guard. The battle was over and he felt as if he had let the weight of the world fall in pieces on the ground. Pieces so small they were like dust.

And now, in the light of day, he felt he was letting go of the anger and disappointment. Maybe, just maybe, it hadn't been just a chance meeting. Perhaps it had been more than a coincidence.

There was something fragile about Jessica, yet something equally strong. She intrigued him. And after hearing her beliefs about parenting, and knowing how they were aligned to his own, she was getting a little further under his skin. Warmth spread through him, along with a stirring in his gut. It felt good but he couldn't ignore that it still caused him a degree of angst.

The woman, pretty as a picture and clearly a competent doctor, while strangely dressed on her first day, was making him second-guess his resolve never to feel anything close to what he felt at that moment. Quickly he realised it wasn't the leftover melancholy of a lonely winter's night, the relief of having the signed custody papers…or the gin from the night before that made him feel that way. It was a Monday morning in a frantic Emergency Department and she was still bringing feelings to the surface that he'd believed he would never, could never, experience again. But was he actually ready for those feelings? Was he prepared to potentially let someone into his life, on whatever level? In the light of day he suddenly wasn't so sure.

'I said, Dr Wainwright, I haven't undertaken the induction yet.'

Harrison pulled his thoughts together and realised by Jessica's response that she was repeating herself. It was ironic that he had been too preoccupied with thoughts of her to hear her words. He was more than a little unnerved. He was never distracted by a woman, let alone while on duty.

'I'm sorry. I was distracted.'

'Yes, I can see that. As I've only seen the ER, I should probably head up and arrange an induction now.'

Harrison paused for the briefest moment, filling his lungs with air. He was worried. He wanted to say that he would be her guide. He wanted very much to take the opportunity to get to know Jessica better, but he hesitated. In almost five years he had not felt attracted to anyone the way he felt himself drawn to the locum Paediatric Consultant. The speed at which he was feeling so comfortable in her presence was disconcerting. He knew he was putting himself at risk but equally he was struggling to deny that he wanted to get to know her a little better. What harm could come of it? he asked himself. They might be great friends, with so much in common.

A simple display of professional politeness, he told himself, but he knew he was lying. There was so much more behind the way he was feeling and it was unsettling but he pushed those fears away as quickly as they surfaced. Once before, he had travelled at a similar speed and he knew the danger signs but this felt very different and he chose to ignore them. It had been a long time ago and, while he still bore the scars, he had an intangible feeling, a feeling deep down inside his gut, that getting to know Dr Jessica Ayers might be worth the risk. He could hear the alarm bells ringing loud and clear and yet he wanted to know more about this woman, take the time to personally show her around the hospital. He was all too aware that he was heading in a direction that was dangerous but something about Jessica was making that very difficult to refuse. He prayed his fears were unfounded.

'I would be happy to show you around, if you like.'

'Really?'

'Yes, really,' he almost laughed.

'That's very kind of you.'

'I like to get to know new staff. Put it down to my curious nature.' Again, he lied but he could hardly admit the truth. 'I'll ask one of the nurses to direct you to HR on the second floor so you can complete any requisite paperwork and then, once you make your way back down here, I'll take you around the rest of the hospital and introduce you to the senior staff.'

'Thank you. That's very nice of you.'

'We're a friendly country bunch here.'

Harrison watched as Jessica considered him for a moment in silence. He suspected that she could see through him but she seemed happy enough.

'I'd appreciate that,' she finally said with a sparkle in the most beautiful green eyes he had ever seen.

Harrison felt himself teetering on the edge of something that he couldn't define but wanted to explore. It was crazy to feel anything for someone so quickly but it felt right. There was a familiarity about Jessica that he couldn't explain or define.

'No doubt you've done most of the paperwork online but occasionally they need a signature in person,' he said, finally breaking the spell under which he felt himself falling. 'The staff will also provide you with a security pass and a designated car park space if you have a car.'

'I do, a rental for six weeks,' Jessica said as she nodded. 'I parked in the general car park this morning.'

'Six weeks?' he asked curiously.

'Yes, I'm covering long service leave for your Paediatric Consultant.'

'Of course.' Harrison physically withdrew as he spoke, taking a step back from Jessica. He was deflated by the news. It had slipped his mind that Jessica's residency was to be so short. Perhaps she might be testing the water, he wondered. Checking if she liked country life, trying it on for size, so to speak. Seeing if she liked the pace of Armidale.

'I have a short lease on the house too. My next position's in Adelaide in seven weeks' time. That role is just four weeks, but fi-fo suits me.'

'Fi-fo?'

'Fly in, fly out.'

'Of course.' Harrison knew he was repeating his words…just as he had almost repeated his mistake of wanting to know a woman passing through town. God, he was doing it again. Hadn't he learnt his lesson? Last time he had stupidly believed the woman who'd married him and had his baby might actually want to stay. And he had been wrong. So very wrong. Nothing could've been further from the truth. He should have known better and this time he had to make sure he did.

'You're filling in for us while Stan Jefferson and his new bride enjoy their honeymoon to

Europe. Some time on the Greek islands and then heading to the French Riviera.'

'So I heard,' she said flatly then continued. 'I mean I knew the purpose of my placement, just not their actual destination. Oh, well, I wish them luck.'

Jessica's monotone, lacklustre reply was not lost on Harrison and his eyes narrowed. Everything he had first assumed about the woman was perhaps not as he had thought. He wasn't expecting her to be gushing about the honeymoon of two people she had never met, but nor had he expected her response to be so devoid of emotion.

'You don't sound too excited for them.'

'I don't know them.'

'That's true.'

Jessica paused. 'Maybe I should have said good luck to them.'

'*Maybe?* That doesn't sound too definite.'

'It's not,' she said, shifting a little on her feet. 'Look, I'm sure the Mediterranean will be superb at this time of year. I'm just…well… you know what—it truly doesn't matter what I think.'

Harrison felt a knot tighten in his gut and a wall rising between them very quickly. She had become almost flippant about the subject and that brought with it a level of concern.

'No, I suppose it doesn't matter what anyone thinks as long as they're happy.' His intuition, together with the cold hard facts, made it clear that Jessica was not the settling-down kind. Not that it bothered him, he reminded himself. He wasn't either now, but it did remind him that he had to keep a professional distance. Jessica had stirred emotions he had forgotten he could feel and he had to rein them in; he felt as if he was stepping into deep waters and he couldn't afford to be swept away. It wasn't something that happened often to him. Quite the opposite—only once before—but, even then, it hadn't been as immediate a connection as he was feeling with Jessica.

Harrison rubbed his chin with his lean fingers. This new side of her seemed cold and detached and abruptly brought back memories of the way his ex-wife had been able to turn her back and walk away from the life he'd thought they would share. And it reminded him that he truly did not read women well at all.

'I'm all about my career. It's my sole focus now and I suspect always will be.'

Harrison had temporarily slipped into a strange space where he had been thinking... Actually, he didn't know what he had been thinking, or feeling, for that matter, but suddenly he realised he should have known better. He felt stupid. Jessica was another career woman. Point-blank. No room for any debate. Her announcement was an unexpected but much needed and timely awakening. It was the cold hard slap back into reality that Harrison knew he needed. He was at least grateful that she was upfront about it. Perhaps his ex-wife had been too but maybe he hadn't looked for the signs back then. He wasn't sure. Perhaps everything that had happened between them had been at such a lightning pace that he couldn't have seen them anyway. With the passing of time came the knowledge that he had to look out for any signs to ensure that he and his son would never be hurt again.

Harrison knew now that he didn't need a woman he found even mildly interesting, let alone intriguing. Certainly not one who wasn't the staying kind. He was doing just fine as a single father and Jessica had brought him to his senses. Being a single parent had sufficient challenges and he knew he didn't need to make it more difficult by letting himself become involved with a woman like her. He had been swept up in a crazy moment he'd thought was serendipity when in fact it was just a distracted locum doctor who had run over his foot. Nothing more. It wasn't a sign of anything other than what it was. An accident. End of story.

No matter how aligned their values and interests had momentarily appeared, they were in fact miles apart. Brick by brick, an impenetrable wall was being erected in his mind. And the construction was happening at breakneck speed. She was everything he didn't need in a woman, all tied up in one beautiful package. Dr Jessica Ayers was heartbreak about to happen for any man who thought long-term or happily ever after. And he wasn't sure why for a split second he might just have been one of those men. He thought he had learnt his lesson and for five years he hadn't thought about love. Then, since meeting Jessica, for some inexplicable reason it had entered his mind again. And he needed to send any thoughts like that packing.

Harrison cleared his throat. 'Actually, I don't think I'll have time today to show you around the hospital after all.'

Jessica's delicately creased brow didn't mask her reaction to his sudden change of heart. 'Is something wrong?'

'No, it's just that I've remembered that I promised to visit a patient later so I won't have time to show you around. I'm sure HR will assign you someone anyway.'

'Of course. I understand…'

'And there's one other thing, Dr Ayers.'

'Jessica,' she corrected him.

'Fine, Jessica.' His eyes narrowed as he spoke. 'As a senior member of the hospital, there is something I need to mention.'

'That sounds serious.'

'Not overly serious, just good professional practice and I think it needs mentioning.'

'Go on,' she said, with the frown slowly creeping over her entire brow.

The tone of Harrison's voice had purposely shifted from warm to aloof. He needed to define their relationship to himself, if no one else. Remind himself that he didn't know the woman standing before him. It didn't matter how almost instantly he had felt a connection. It wasn't real. They were just feelings passing through his mind, just as she was passing through town. Both would be gone in the blink of an eye.

Jessica had folded her arms across her delicate frame. She was preparing for a fight. The irony was that the battle was an internal one, actually going on inside Harrison. His actions were all about setting personal boundaries that he suddenly felt he needed.

'Professionally speaking, I have to tell you that you should have cleared it with me before you acted in any capacity in the ER since you hadn't officially started.' He paused to regroup his thoughts and stay on track. 'There's no delicate way to put it, Jessica, except to say it how it is. You overstepped the mark and I hope it doesn't happen again.'

CHAPTER FIVE

JESSICA FELT THE wind being knocked out of her sails. She had stepped up to help out. She'd hardly expected a medal but she also hadn't expected a dressing-down about it. She could understand if he had called her on her unprofessional attire. That was very real in her mind. But he'd made no reference to her clothing at all, focusing on her stepping in to help.

Could the man have a twin brother? she asked herself silently as she dropped her gaze. If not, then she surmised she must be quite delusional to have thought of him as kind or charismatic in any way. He was abrupt at best and plain rude if she was to be honest with herself. She found herself in a situation that felt so unsettling she wanted to exit as soon as possible. She felt like a teenager being reprimanded. Again, she realised she was a terrible judge of character.

Not that it came as a surprise to her but she had hoped she had improved over time. Clearly not.

Nothing had changed, not her nor the men she found herself drawn to on any level, however fleetingly.

Jessica wasn't sure what to say. Her thoughts ran the gamut from a transfer to another hospital to eating an entire tub of chocolate ice cream or perhaps having a stiff drink at the end of her shift. All of them would solve the problem in very different ways and all were overly dramatic but that was how she felt. Her judgement, she accepted, was below poor before she'd arrived in Armidale but Dr Harrison Wainwright had, in a few minutes, convinced her that her personality assessment skills were hitting a new low. How and why she had even for the briefest moment thought that the man was worthy of head space before she'd fallen asleep the night before was nonsensical.

Drawing breath, she gathered her thoughts. They were threadbare at best. He was condescending in his approach. As a fully qualified professional, she had stepped up to help out. How dare he speak to her that way? She should have taken another role. There was no shortage of locum positions and if she had gone elsewhere there would be no Dr Wainwright and she would be wearing a suit and not something she felt more suited to the stables than a hospital. Alternatively, she could have taken the day off to wait for her clothes and blamed the airline. But no, she'd turned up feeling like Little Orphan Annie, helped out and got a telling-off for stepping up.

She was embarrassed for the third time in his presence. Twice that day and once the day before at the airport. *Three strikes and you're out*, she told herself as she nodded and walked away without saying a word. But in this case he was the one out.

Of any, ever so fleeting, romantic musings she might have harboured for him.

'Dr Ayers,' the hospital orderly called down the corridor to Jessica. It was almost two-thirty by then. Jessica had undertaken her induction and then begun rounds on the Paediatric ward. Getting to know the nursing staff and her little patients had been her priority.

'Yes,' she said and turned to find the young man tugging her suitcases behind him.

'They told me to find you as these were urgent.'

Jessica couldn't remember ever feeling as relieved and happy as she did at that moment and she had no intention of hiding her elation.

'Oh, my God, thank you so much!' she said as she rushed towards him as if he might disappear with the suitcases as magically as he had appeared.

'No problem,' he replied and released his hold on the bags. 'Apparently they missed the first flight and made it onto the second one.'

'You have no idea how happy this makes me.'

'I think I do,' he smirked before turning back the way he had entered the Paediatric ward.

Jessica could see by his expression that her reaction had been a little over the top but she didn't bother to explain. There was no point. She was happy and had told him as much.

Now she could get dressed and forget her Farmer Jane entree into the hospital had ever happened. What she couldn't forget was Dr Harrison Wainwright's curt and unexpected call on her helping out earlier. It had played on her mind. She really hadn't pegged him for being so rigid and black and white about a situation. Processes were important within a hospital but she had only been trying to help.

Stupidly, she'd thought he had appeared very nice at the airport. Almost chivalrous, she mused as she wheeled her suitcases past the nurses' station, telling them she was changing and would be back in fifteen minutes. And watching him triage and manage the young pregnant patient so compassionately, and then listening to him speak so encouragingly to the medical student had led her to believe he was a decent human being. Then abruptly he had changed and called her out. It was ridiculous.

Men had a habit of doing that around her, she realised. One minute they're single, then the next they're married. In this case, one minute Harrison was a charming, lovely man and the next quite abrupt and rude. His behaviour was odd at best and it had made her realise that her first impression couldn't have been more wrong. She was strangely relieved and almost grateful, she decided as she closed her office door, that he was not the man she'd first thought. If he had been, it might have been a problem. But not any more.

She shook her head, appalled by her borderline hormonal reaction to him, as she unlocked her suitcase and pulled out a pale pink turtleneck sweater and navy trousers that she was relieved to see weren't creased. Although, even if they had been, she would have still worn them.

Focus on what's important, she reminded herself as she tried to stop her thoughts returning to the man who had just delivered her a harsh reality check. Her shoes were in the other suitcase so she quickly closed the first and unlocked the second one that was already lying flat on the floor. Her tights were in a separate compartment and easy to find and she quickly changed.

'Finally,' she sighed as she closed the door to her office and returned to the job at hand.

Her tiny patients and their families. And not her stupid daydreams of a man she barely knew—someone who behaved so erratically it had dropped her belief in her own judgement lower than it had already been. *I'd like to show you around the hospital... Actually, come to think of it, no, I won't. Instead I'll tell you off for unprofessional behaviour.* It didn't make sense but it did help her to rein in her emotions. It was all about her professional reputation. She was grateful that the ER Consultant had, so less than eloquently, reminded her she was done and dusted with giving men the time of day. Her walls were back up and no one was getting close. Any interest in Harrison was gone and she silently thanked him and the universe as she collected the file for her next patient.

Jessica had visited all but one of the patients in the twenty-eight-bed Paediatric ward. Six-year-old Chloe Naughton was the last. She had taken considerably longer with each patient than she would ordinarily but Armidale Hospital was nothing like the busy city wards she had experienced. Between the high number of agency nursing staff and patients from all over, there had been few connections outside the immediate patient-medical staff relationship, with little known about the patient's background if it wasn't on the notes. However, this hospital was very family-centric and the nurses knew almost all the family members, and the paramedics, Jessica remembered from the morning. The community spirit was evident in the close relationships between everyone at the hospital, no matter in what capacity.

It felt good, she admitted, but she knew she had to keep to herself. She wasn't staying and she didn't want to settle in and start feeling too comfortable and risk wanting to stay. That was not an option. When the time came she would leave and start again somewhere else.

'Chloe arrived in the ER two days ago,' the nurse, Rosie, began—she had just started her shift. 'She was convulsing at home and lost consciousness in the ambulance.'

'She's been diagnosed with diabetes, I see.'

'Yes, Dr Ayers,' Rosie responded as the two

of them stood outside the patient's room in the corridor so they could speak candidly about the little girl. 'Dr Wainwright ran blood tests and found autoantibodies that are common in type one diabetes, as opposed to type two. Chloe also had ketones in her urine sample so type one diabetes was his diagnosis.'

Dr Wainwright? Of course, Jessica thought. He would have been in ER and been the first point of contact for the family.

'Did you follow up with a glycated haemoglobin test?' Jessica asked as she searched the notes for the answer to her question.

'Yes. Dr Wainwright ordered it when he transferred her to Paediatrics in the afternoon. And the blood test provided us with the average blood sugar level for Chloe for the past two to three months. The percentage of blood sugar attached to the oxygen-carrying protein in the red blood cells was extremely high.'

'I can see here it was close to seven per cent on two separate tests,' Jessica commented as her eyes found what she was looking for. Harrison had been thorough and left nothing to chance. This reinforced that, while he might be a pig of a man, he was a good doctor.

'Any family history?' Jessica enquired as she looked over at the little girl sleeping on the bed while her mother held her hand.

'Paternal grandfather.'

'How are the family taking the news?'

'Not good at all, unfortunately. Her mother, Rachel, hasn't left her side since she was admitted. Chloe is an IVF baby, conceived after five failed rounds. A very wanted and loved little girl.'

'And the child's father; how is he reacting? I hope he's not feeling any sense of guilt over the genetics. It may not be inherited from his side alone.'

'Chloe's father, Sam, was killed in a farm accident a little over six months ago.'

'Oh, my God, I'm so sorry to hear that.'

'It's been a traumatic time for the family,' Rosie replied. 'Sam was ten years older than his wife, in his mid forties when he passed. Rachel's only thirty-five and financially she's going to be okay, emotionally not so much. She's been dealing with the grief of losing

Sam, so this has been another blow to her fragile state.'

Jessica paused before she answered. 'She certainly has a lot to manage emotionally. No wonder she hasn't left her daughter's side.'

'We put Chloe in a private room so Rachel can sleep on a roll-out bed.'

'Has a counsellor been to see her?'

'Yes, she has and Dr Wainwright has visited two or three times a day as well. He brings a sandwich or a cup of coffee for Rachel when he comes in. Sam Naughton was like Dr Wainwright's big brother as he grew up. He kept a watchful eye over him so he's returning the favour now.'

Jessica drew in a breath. She really didn't want to hear anything about Harrison. *Complex* appeared to be an understatement about the man. And *close-knit* was equally an understatement about the town.

She pushed thoughts of Harrison aside and focused on the situation at hand. The family had dealt with significant tragedy in a very short timeframe. She wanted to provide hope but she wasn't going to be able to paint a perfect picture or sugar-coat anything. Chloe's condition was serious and, if not managed properly, it could be potentially life-threatening. Chloe needed to be everyone's first priority at this moment.

Chloe's mother lifted her head as Jessica and Rosie approached.

'Hello, Mrs Naughton,' Jessica said softly and extended her hand. 'I'm Dr Ayers, the new Paediatric Consultant, and I'll be looking after your daughter until she is stabilised and can go home in your care.'

'Pleased to meet you, Doctor,' the woman replied, the rims of her eyes still red from rubbing away tears. She was about Jessica's age but her vulnerable state made her appear younger than that.

Jessica felt her heart melt a little, the way it always did and had done from day one. She hadn't liked the feeling as an intern but she was told by one of her mentors early in her career that the day she lost that compassion and empathy was the day she should leave the profession. She always repeated his words in her head when she felt herself struggling with the sadness faced by the families of her tiny patients.

'Chloe's sleeping so perhaps we can step away and I can answer any questions you might have about her treatment plan?'

'I don't want to leave in case she wakes.'

'We can check if Rosie or one of the other nurses can stay with her…' Jessica began.

'Don't bother the nursing staff. They're busy so I'll stay,' a deep male voice echoed behind them. 'You know for a fact that Chloe loves her godfather. And I don't get enough time with her. I haven't seen her at all today because ER's been like a train station, as Dr Ayers knows first-hand.'

Jessica knew the voice. It was Harrison. She didn't need to turn and face him. His voice and the last words he'd spoken to her still rang in her mind. She was confused and didn't want to give him another thought but he was making that very difficult. Her focus was on her patient's mother but his presence was difficult to ignore.

'Are you sure? Aren't you busy in the ER, Harrison?' Rachel asked as she gently prised her fingers free of her daughter's hand, placing it under the soft blanket before she stood up to greet him.

'Never too busy for my two favourite girls,' he told her.

Jessica turned to see the two embrace and a tear trickle down Rachel's cheek. The young mother wiped the tear away as she stepped back and sat down next to her daughter, turning away from him. Jessica suspected it was to prevent him from seeing her crying. Harrison reached into his pocket and handed her his handkerchief over her shoulder. He hadn't missed Rachel's tears or perhaps if he had missed seeing them he had guessed they would follow. He was once again morphing into the gallant man she had met the day before at the airport. Confusion was reigning supreme at that moment but she had to push it aside yet again.

'Please, Rachel,' he continued. 'If you won't do it for yourself, then do it for Chloe. You need to step away and recharge. It's overwhelming in here, not to mention the fact you need to eat. Even if it's cafeteria food, you need to grab something before you fade away.'

Jessica suspected the casual tone in his voice was masking his own concern at the situation. He knew the results of the tests and was aware of Chloe's condition but was clearly responding with Rachel's emotional state at the forefront. The young mother had already dealt with so much, after so many failed attempts to have a baby and recently losing her husband, and he was treading carefully. Jessica's respect for the man standing so close caught her by surprise.

She watched as he leant in and spoke softly. 'I'm serious, Rachel. Take half an hour to grab a coffee and a sandwich downstairs. Maybe Dr Ayers can join you and you can go through the treatment plan in the cafeteria.'

'I'm not sure...' Rachel began.

'Don't make me call in the heavy guns...' Harrison cut in.

'My mother?'

'You got it. I have her number on speed-dial.'

His lips curved into a grin and Jessica was annoyed that it was an appealing grin.

'She's driving down from Brisbane today to be with us anyway, so you can't use that threat, but I am starting to feel hungry.'

'Good, and I could do with a coffee and a sandwich so you'd be doing me a favour too,' Jessica cut in, wanting to help Rachel and eager to leave Harrison's presence. 'I've not had anything to eat since breakfast.'

'Okay, but I'll only be a few minutes, tops,' Rachel said, climbing tentatively to her feet and lifting her bag onto her shoulder. 'I promise, ten minutes at most and I'll be back.'

'Take thirty. I'll still be here when you get back,' he said as he looked towards Jessica with a guilty expression. 'I want to apologise before you leave, Dr Ayers. Your willingness to jump in and help out was admirable and I was out of place for calling you on it. I'm sorry if I was rude. No, not *if* I was rude—I *was* rude; that's not up for debate.'

'What are you taking about, Harrison?' Rachel asked, tilting her head.

'I'm apologising to Dr Ayers. I behaved poorly earlier in ER.'

'You, rude? You've never been rude to anyone in the whole time I've known you.'

'I guess there's a first time for everything and, unfortunately for me, it was this morning.'

Jessica felt the weight of two sets of eyes fall upon her. She wanted to say that she would not accept his apology and she wanted nothing much to do with the man. Ever again. But she couldn't. She had to accept Harrison's apology as politely as he had offered it. Perhaps his behaviour had been as out of character as her dress sense that morning, which to her surprise neither Harrison or anyone else at the hospital had mentioned. There had been no judgement on that level from anyone, just herself. She started to wonder if she was her own biggest critic. She wasn't sure but at that moment she knew she had to respond courteously and work out the truth later about herself…and Harrison.

'Accepted,' Jessica finally announced. 'Now, let's get you downstairs for something to eat.'

She wanted to dismiss any thoughts she was having about Harrison. She didn't need any complications. Giving her best to the patients for the next six weeks was her priority. Nothing else.

'Okay, but promise me, Harrison, that you'll call me if Chloe stirs.'

'I'll call you *and* page Dr Ayers, I promise.'

Harrison saluted as he sat down and took Chloe's tiny hand in his and brushed a wisp of her golden locks from her pale as porcelain forehead.

And against her will and every wall she had tirelessly erected, he was threatening to once again break them down.

'How would you like your coffee, Mrs Naughton?'

'White, no sugar, and please call me Rachel.'

Jessica left Rachel sitting at the table and approached the counter of the hospital cafeteria. As she stood in the short queue looking back at the table, she watched Rachel looking off to a faraway place. She wondered if the young woman was thinking about her husband, about the plans they'd made to have a family and raise them in Armidale. And about the five babies they had lost on their journey to have the precious little girl who was now lying on the hospital bed. It all seemed so unfair and, compared to her own heartbreak, Rachel's was so much worse. It suddenly put things in perspective, as work always did for Jessica.

She could only imagine the pain and worry that would be consuming Chloe's mother. Jessica knew she had to deliver the good and the bad news but it had to be done in a manner that would not threaten Rachel's already tenuous hold on her emotions.

Finally, she made it to the front of the lunch line and ordered two white coffees and two mixed sandwiches. She reached into her suit pocket to pay at the register.

'It's covered already,' came the rosy-faced woman's thick Scottish reply. 'Dr Wainwright's paid for it.'

'But how?'

'He called down and told me to put it on his tab.'

'Okay, then please put *one* coffee and *one*

sandwich on his tab,' Jessica continued, taking money from her wallet and handing it over. 'I'll pay for my own.'

'I think you'd best accept Dr Wainwright's kind offer. It's only a wee sandwich and coffee, which, by the way, is going cold, and there's some other lovely people waiting to be served,' the woman said as she gently pushed the tray in Jessica's direction and smiled. 'I think you'll like your sandwiches. I made them fresh this morning.'

Jessica gave up. Time was precious and she needed to sit down and speak with Rachel. It was just a coffee and *wee* sandwich after all, she reminded herself. In the scheme of things, it wasn't worth fussing over and perhaps it was his way of cementing his apology.

She balanced the tray on the edge of the table while she transferred both coffees and sandwiches to the table top.

'Thank you,' Rachel said, glancing at the food but not rushing to have any of it.

'Lunch is Dr Wainwright's treat; he called down and covered it.'

'He's such a sweetheart.'

Jessica couldn't help but shake her head a little as she looked away and rested the tray on a spare seat. *Was he?* She was quite confused—and she hated being confused. She was starting to think that maybe she had actually overstepped the mark and should have sought approval before stepping up in the ER earlier. Was Harrison just being responsible and following protocol and she was being the defensive one? Perhaps her past was impacting on the way she saw everyone. It could be that she was looking for a reason to dislike the man.

It didn't matter. Whether Harrison was the salt of the earth or arrogant bore no relevance. She was done trying to work out men's intentions or personalities. She was just done with the lot of them.

'He's been my rock since my husband died. I don't know what I would've done without him. He took charge of everything, even organising and paying for the funeral. I didn't want him to do it; we had enough savings and my husband had life insurance, but Harrison said he wanted me to keep that tucked away for Chloe's education. He insisted, not in an overbearing way, more a caring big brother way. He's taken on the role of Chloe's godfather very seriously. But that's Harrison. When he commits, he gives it a hundred per cent.'

Jessica had to admit that his management of the ER did reflect that same philosophy. He was clearly a man who wasn't half-hearted or casual about anything. He was a puzzle she didn't expect or think she was equipped to face.

'My life was a blur,' Rachel continued, bringing Jessica back to reality. 'I truly didn't know which way was up and which down. I was drowning in disbelief, shock, worry, all of it, so Harrison stepped in and let me just look after Chloe and myself without the additional burden of the arrangements.'

Jessica nodded. The fact that Harrison had stepped up for Rachel and Chloe when Sam had died was indisputable, just as Jessica's immediate and unexpected attraction to the man was undeniable. But neither mattered now. The task at hand was preparing Rachel for the journey ahead in managing Chloe's illness. Her personal feelings about anything or anyone would, as they always did, take a back seat at this time.

'I can answer your questions about Chloe's ongoing treatment while we eat if you like,' Jessica told her to change the subject.

Rachel nodded and then picked up her coffee and took a sip. 'Thank you.'

'Ask anything you need to know and don't hold back. If for some reason I don't know the answer, I will find out.'

Rachel sat in silence for a moment, her eyes wandering again to somewhere in the distance. Jessica unwrapped her sandwich and took a small bite of the wholemeal bread and vegetarian filling.

'Will my daughter die?' Rachel suddenly asked. Her voice was shaky.

Jessica's hands dropped quietly with her sandwich onto her plate and once again she drew a breath. The question was honest but confronting. So the answer needed to be the same, but tempered with enough bedside manner to not cause unnecessary grief or worry.

'No, not if we manage her condition correctly,' Jessica returned after a moment. She was aware of everything that had transpired in Rachel's life in the past twelve months and, prior to that, with the loss of the other babies and knew the woman needed hope in her life. 'And we have to do that to the absolute best of our ability until Chloe's old enough to manage it herself—and then to see that she does the same. *Never* forgetting the seriousness of her condition is the key to Chloe having a healthy and fulfilling life.'

'But what if we get it wrong? What if we miss something…? I don't know…mess up somehow? What then?'

'We won't. Medical research is advanced and we know what medications are the most effective and we'll have a treatment plan that ensures Chloe's condition does not deteriorate.'

'But what about the times when she's not with me?' Rachel asked, firing another question about yet another scenario and not hiding how scared she was feeling. Her fear was escalating and Jessica could see she was becoming more overwhelmed by the minute.

'You will educate family and friends and, most importantly, Chloe herself so, for those times you're not with her, she's still safe,' Jessica continued in a calming manner. 'And you want your daughter to enjoy increasing independence as she grows up and, with that independence, comes responsibility for making the right choices.'

'And if she doesn't. What will happen then?'

'She could become seriously ill.' There was no easy way around that question. Choosing honesty was the only response. If Chloe was not responsible as she grew older then the outlook was not good. 'But you don't need to consider that at the moment. You have a six-year-old daughter who is going to learn to adapt. Just as you will.'

Jessica watched Rachel slump a little further into her chair.

'Chloe will fully understand the disease as she grows up and, with a healthy respect for herself, she will ensure she does not take unnecessary risks. It's about balance and each day she will be faced with choices that ordinary children don't have to consider but Chloe will know that she needs to factor in her diabetes.'

'It's a big ask of a little girl.'

'It's a big ask of her mother too but you'll both step up. I have no doubt that your daughter will be as strong as you've been for a long time now.'

Jessica watched as Rachel took another sip of her coffee.

'Please eat something,' Jessica said kindly but with a level of firmness as a health professional. Her eyes travelled down to the uneaten sandwich still on Rachel's plate. 'You'll be no use to Chloe when she needs you if you're rundown and get sick from both worry and lack of nutrition.'

'I guess,' came Rachel's muttered reply before she took a few tiny bites of the sandwich.

Jessica followed suit but there weren't any bite-size mouthfuls. She was hungry and wolfed down the sandwich and coffee in a few minutes. It had been hours since breakfast.

'Would you like me to explain the disease in more depth—and the treatment plan?' Jessica asked as she swallowed the last rushed mouthful.

'Yes. I need to know everything. And as soon as possible.'

Jessica dabbed her mouth with the paper napkin and began. 'With diabetes, a treatment plan is a *lifelong* treatment plan. It may alter over the course of time but it will be a continuous plan, as we will be treating Chloe's diabetes not curing it. Right now, there's no cure for the disease but that's not to say there won't be a cure one day.'

'But she can live a long healthy life, can't she?'

'Most definitely. With proper care, Chloe will look and feel as healthy as any girl her age. And live a long life.'

Jessica watched as Rachel shifted in her seat, her posture improving with the optimistic prognosis. Jessica had never wanted to add to Rachel's stress; however, she did need to explain the seriousness of Chloe's chronic illness.

'Chloe's treatment plan will be based on her

very specific needs and the hospital will also provide a diabetes healthcare team.'

'So not just you then, Dr Ayers?'

'No. I'm just standing in for the resident paediatrician's leave. He'll be back in six weeks and, together with a number of medical professionals across the hospital, he will provide advice and support,' Jessica told her, unsure of the identity of the individuals, though she knew the various medical specialties who would be represented in a hospital of that size. 'But, before we get to the team's role, let me explain a little about the illness and the treatment plan.'

Rachel nodded and took another bite of the egg and rocket sandwich.

'Treatment is never the same for every child or adult. The types of insulin given and the schedules for giving insulin each day vary between patients.'

'So Chloe will need an injection of insulin every day?'

'Yes.'

'For ever?'

'Yes. This illness is not something that

Chloe will grow out of. It will be something she manages for life.' Jessica paused for a moment. 'I'm sorry that I'm giving you so much to think about now. I thought that it all would have been explained to you yesterday.'

'It was, and I know diabetes is a lifelong condition,' Rachel replied with a look of sheer exhaustion crossing her drawn face. 'I was just too emotional to take anything much in. It washed over me like a tidal wave and I just tried to keep my head above water and focus on Chloe's immediate needs and not break down in front of her.'

'That's understandable,' Jessica reassured her. 'You're doing an amazing job. I'll let you know what's important for now and the rest can wait. I'm mindful you'll want to head back to Chloe.'

And no doubt Dr Wainwright would need to head back down to the ER, she mused. And she wanted to give him a wide berth. Spending as little time with him as possible was her aim for the time she had in Armidale. She feared that he could complicate her life unnecessarily. She prayed he would leave the minute they arrived back in Chloe's room and she could avoid any further awkwardness.

'Harrison did promise he would send a text if she woke,' Rachel replied before she took a deep and worried breath that filled her lungs then deflated just as quickly. 'I think I'm in a better mind-set today. Do you have the time to explain everything to me? I worry that Harrison might leave something out so I don't worry. But I need to know everything.'

Jessica had the remainder of the afternoon free, so she could afford the time. And she didn't care to spend any more time than necessary with Dr Wainwright so she was happy to tell Rachel everything she needed to know.

'Chloe will need insulin to manage her blood glucose level,' Jessica began. 'The blood glucose level is the amount of glucose in the blood.'

'So, is insulin all she needs or are there other things we need to do and how will we manage this when she starts school?'

'If there is a school nurse or first aid officer, they could help until Chloe can do it herself,' Jessica said as she met Rachel's gaze levelly.

'And the hospital will provide ongoing assistance.'

Rachel nodded but didn't look convinced.

'I do feel better knowing I'm not left alone to deal with everything,' she said as she picked some stray alfalfa shoots from her plate and nibbled on them.

'You must ask for additional support if you need it,' Jessica said firmly. 'You can't go it alone on this, Rachel.'

The young woman nodded. 'I won't, I promise. And with all that assistance, I won't have to rely on Harrison as much in the future.'

The mention of his name brought a little knot rushing back to Jessica's stomach.

'He needs a life too. He has a lot on his plate to manage—he doesn't need me on top of everything else,' Rachel continued with a wistful smile. 'He's such a wonderful man and he needs to find someone to share his life and he can't do that if he concentrates on helping me.'

Jessica swallowed. The last thing she wanted to hear was that Harrison Wainwright was eligible and apparently not as dreadful as she had come to believe. On top of the fact he was also, from first impressions in the ER, a highly skilled doctor with a genuinely kind and understanding bedside manner to children and adults alike. All the ingredients for a disaster when she was, for some unknown reason, feeling vulnerable around him.

Suddenly Jessica had been catapulted out of her comfort zone. And she was nervous.

Of him…and of her own feelings.

CHAPTER SIX

THE NEXT FEW days passed quickly. Jessica did her best to avoid Harrison. Her patient load kept her in Paediatrics and away from ER. She passed him in the corridor once or twice, acknowledging him with a polite nod. It was working for her and she hoped to keep it that way for as long as possible. The nights were a little different because, for reasons not understood by Jessica, his face wandered into her mind just before she fell asleep. Every night.

She had almost succeeded in making it to the end of day four without being too close to the handsome medico until he happened upon her in Chloe's room when the little girl was being released into her mother's care.

'Now, you have the hospital number and the individual numbers for each of the diabetic healthcare team,' Jessica told her as she signed the hospital discharge papers and gave them to Rosie.

'Yes,' Rachel answered, patting her oversized handbag. 'It's all in here.'

Jessica watched as Rachel lifted Chloe onto her hip. The little girl clung to her like a baby koala.

'You're going to be fine, both of you. We have a district nurse calling in tomorrow to check up on how you're progressing so you don't have to unsettle Chloe by bringing her back here.'

'Don't forget about me,' Harrison's voice boomed from across the room.

Jessica turned to see his tall silhouette in the doorway. His white consulting coat couldn't hide his muscular physique. The shapeless coat was hanging open but he had a caramel-coloured fine-knit sweater that skimmed and accentuated his toned body. Navy trousers and brown loafers completed the picture that Jessica wished she was not witnessing.

'It's Uncle Harry, Chloe,' Rachel said happily. 'He's come to say goodbye.'

'Is he going on a trip?'

'No.' Rachel laughed as she looked her daughter in the eyes. 'We are. Well, sort of... We're going home. And he'll visit us there soon, I'm sure.'

'Bye, Uncle Harry,' the little girl muttered, then put her thumb back in her mouth and nestled against the warmth of her mother's chest.

Harrison crossed the room with long purposeful steps that covered the space quickly. And with each step Jessica felt the air escaping and her face becoming flushed. She took a few steps back. She was finding the room a little close, and suddenly it became difficult to breathe.

'I will visit you on the weekend. I promise,' he told her and kissed the top of her head before he took a small step back and gently turned her to fully face him. 'Now, you need to be a good girl, the best, in fact, and get lots of rest and do just what Mummy says.'

'Do I have to have needles every day, Uncle Harry?'

Harrison paused for a moment and his gaze wandered over to Jessica. It took her by surprise that he looked a little lost. She'd never expected to see that expression and it tugged at her heart.

'Yes,' Jessica said, moving closer to the three of them again. It was instinctive for her to save him. He was Chloe's godfather and she felt the need to remove the pressure from him. Pressure that he oddly didn't seem to be coping with at that moment. Jessica needed to be the one to deliver the bad news and he could be the one to console the little girl. It was almost as if they had unintentionally adopted aunt and uncle roles.

'But it hurts.'

'I know it does, Chloe. But it's only for a minute and then the little stinging feeling goes away—and you need the medicine to stay healthy and run around like the other children. And Mummy needs you to be healthy so you can help her around the house too. I bet you're a big help.'

'I make my bed and I feed our cat, Snowflake, and—' Chloe paused and her eyes glanced from side to side '—and I give the hens water. We have seven girl hens but no boy hens because they're noisy and wake us up in the morning,' she continued, shaking her tiny head. 'The boys in my class at school are like that too. They're so noisy.'

Jessica smiled at the little girl's words and continued, 'Boys can be noisy and seven hens must keep you busy. And making your bed and feeding Snowflake are all things that Mummy needs help with. If you aren't well because you've not had your medicine, then she'll have to do all of it and—'

'She'll get tired and cry again, like when Daddy died,' the little girl cut in.

Jessica fell silent. She wasn't sure what to say. She had been blindsided by the honesty of Chloe's words. Rachel's emotional state and the recent loss of her husband had momentarily been forgotten in the fuss over Chloe.

Instantly, as if he knew that Jessica was searching for the right thing to say, Harrison cut in. It was a tag team that Jessica hadn't expected to be a part of at all.

'Yes, Chloe. Mummy might get tired and mummies cry when they are tired and sad, so you must try your best to be strong. But if you have days when you're not strong, then you get

Mummy to call me and I can help you to look after the cat and the hens. I'm only ten minutes away from the farm,' he told her.

Jessica looked over at Harrison, just as he turned to her. It was a knowing look. A look of gratitude and something more…something that Jessica couldn't quite define.

'Let's get the pair of you out of here and back home before the rain hits,' Rosie added, breaking the moment as she attempted to bustle Rachel and Chloe out of the room.

Jessica wasn't sure if she was relieved or disappointed. But she was confused that she didn't know how she felt. Of that she was certain.

'I'll take you down to Reception to complete the paperwork,' the nurse continued as the three of them headed out, leaving Jessica and Harrison alone.

'Again, I'm sorry about the other day,' Harrison said, running his hand over his forehead. 'You stepped up and, instead of thanking you, I told you off. It was wrong of me. I guess I'm accustomed to running things and I was taken aback. But that's no excuse.'

'You've apologised already and I've accepted. Let's leave it at that,' Jessica responded, eager to get away from the man who was making her pulse race and her heart flutter when she wanted to harbour some sort of negative feelings towards him. It wasn't a fleeting interest that had passed, as she had hoped. Just being near him was causing a reaction that unsettled her. And she didn't want or need to be having that sort of reaction. She didn't need any complications during her short stay in Armidale. She wanted to keep it purely professional and keep him at arm's length. No unnecessary chit-chat, no reason to learn more about him and, as a result, find him even more attractive than she did already. An apologetic handsome man was the absolute last thing on her wish list.

'All righty,' he said, looking taken aback by her dismissive response to his apology.

Jessica immediately felt terrible, suddenly worried that she was now the one overreacting. It was ridiculous that she cared what he thought but she did again. It was all beyond her comprehension and confusing and yet she felt compelled to step in and save it.

'Now it's my turn to apologise. I'm sorry. I—'

Their pagers both went off at the same time, cutting short her words. They looked down simultaneously and saw they were being called to the ER.

'Dr Wainwright, Dr Ayers—' a young ER nurse rushed into the room '—I know you've been paged but I thought I could brief you on the way down. There's been an accident on the New England Highway. A school bus left the road. Four ambulances are on their way here now. Nine seriously injured, eleven others with minor injuries and an unspecified number with cuts and abrasions that are being treated at the scene but may be transported here later. ETA eight minutes.'

'The driver?' Harrison asked as he and Jessica followed the nurse to the lift.

'Pronounced dead at the scene.'

Jessica sighed and closed her eyes for the briefest moment as they all stepped into the lift. 'From injuries sustained in the accident?'

'No, it appears he suffered a heart attack and died at the wheel; that's why the bus left the road,' the nurse continued as the lift reached the ground floor and they all stepped out in unison and headed to the ER. 'He called out to both the teachers as he clasped his chest and tried to keep control of the bus. In the statement to police, the paramedics overheard one teacher say the driver had done his absolute best to slow the bus, but at such a high speed he couldn't prevent them leaving the road. The teachers were at the rear of the bus and couldn't get to the driver in time to take the wheel.'

'What a tragic set of circumstances,' Jessica said solemnly as they entered the doors of the ER.

'Do you have an idea of the age range of the children?' Harrison asked as he scrubbed and donned surgical gloves and gown.

'It was two year five classes on an excursion, so the students are all around nine to ten years of age.'

Jessica followed suit and scrubbed and gowned. 'And the extent of the injuries?'

'Two suspected spinal cord injuries, multiple fractures, lacerations and all are being monitored for internal bleeding.'

'Any fatalities other than the driver?'

'Not yet.'

'Let's make sure we have all bays emptied if possible,' Harrison called out to the ER staff. 'Any non-life-threatening can be triaged to a waiting room. Stat. We have less than two minutes to ETA.'

Jessica watched as four patients were wheeled on their beds out of ER and other beds were quickly wheeled in by orderlies. She suspected that the experienced ER staff had already made that decision and the triaging was well underway before she and Harrison arrived. It was like clockwork and far too quick to have been arranged on his command. They just knew what they needed to do. It was a well-oiled machine that Harrison ran.

One minute later, and one minute ahead of schedule, two stretchers were rushed into the ER. Jessica could see immediately these were two of the serious injuries. Both were in neck braces and bandages had been applied to their heads and one had both legs in splints. A man in his early forties was walking beside one of them. Jessica assumed he was one of the children's teachers. She walked into bay five with the first and Harrison took the second stretcher into bay four.

'Nine-year-old male. Suspected fractures to both legs, potential neck injury and blunt head trauma from hitting the seat in front and being thrown to the ground on impact. No seat belt. We inserted an IV en route and administered pain relief as he was experiencing pain while conscious. While his injuries are extensive, there's no sign of internal bleeding and the pain would indicate no C1-C2 vertebrae damage. He's on a board and we braced him as a precaution.'

'Great job and it does sound promising,' Jessica replied. 'Let's transfer him onto the bed.'

The paramedics and the nurses worked swiftly and carefully to execute the transfer, keeping the board in place before they handed over their notes and exited the bay with the stretcher.

'His name is Trevor Saunders,' the man

added. 'I'm his teacher, Gavin Watson. We were on an excursion to Armidale from the Tamworth Elementary School.'

Moments later, two more stretchers arrived with paramedics and they were taken into the adjacent bays, with a third stretcher and two more paramedics following closely behind and being parked in the final empty bay. All nurses and ER staff were engaged and Jessica was aware there were four more serious cases en route.

'Have you been assessed by the paramedics, Mr Watson?' Jessica asked before she donned a surgical mask and approached the child.

'I was assessed at the accident site by paramedics and cleared. My seat belt was in place, just as I thought the students' belts were because we have a school travel policy and strict rules. Unfortunately, the boys thought they knew better and I had no way to see they had undone their seat belts just before the accident.'

'Would you be able to help identify the students we are treating? If you make your way over to the desk and explain what you have been asked to do, one of the nurses at the desk will help you. Please stay close so we can call on you if we need anything further,' Jessica said in short staccato sentences. 'I assume the parents have been contacted?'

The teacher nodded. 'My colleague, Ms Forbes, is still at the accident scene with those students not hurt in the accident and the school has called all of the parents,' he said before following her instructions and making his way to the ER desk.

Quickly Jessica turned her attention back to the young patient, who was unconscious but breathing steadily. 'Trevor,' she began in a soft and soothing voice. 'My name is Jessica and I'm a doctor. While you cannot see me, you may be able to hear me. You were in an accident and you've been brought to the Armidale Hospital, about an hour and a half from your school in Tamworth.'

There was no visible reaction to her words.

'We are going to put some monitors on you. If you can hear me, you need to stay very still. You hurt your back and your legs when the bus left the road so we don't want you trying to move.'

The nurses worked quickly to ensure the boy's heart, temperature and breathing were all monitored.

'BP is rising—it's now ninety over forty-five,' the nurse announced, then continued as she looked over the paramedic's notes. 'En route it was eighty over forty.'

The boy's eyelids began to flicker. Jessica could see he was regaining consciousness.

'Welcome back, Trevor.'

His eyes closed again and the flickering stopped for a moment.

'The patient is drifting in and out of consciousness. I need a portal X-ray machine to assess the damage to the lower limbs,' she told one of the nurses in the same calm but lowered voice. 'According to the notes, we have a suspected fracture of right tibia and left femur but the issue for me is the potential for spinal cord injury.'

'BP's a little higher again and oxygen saturation is improving,' the nurse reported.

'Good, his pain must be under control but

there's still a risk of lumbar spinal cord damage if he moves so let's not get ahead of ourselves.'

Jessica confirmed the reading on the monitor out of habit and felt silently pleased and confident that she was not dealing with a quadriplegia diagnosis.

The young boy began to open his eyes and they remained open for a few seconds.

'Trevor, I know you are feeling confused and maybe a little scared but you're safe. You're in a hospital and your parents are on their way now to be with you. I'm not sure if you could hear me when you first arrived but my name is Jessica and I'm a doctor.'

The nurse leant in to Jessica and said in a low whisper, 'They left Tamworth twenty minutes ago so their ETA is around an hour.'

'Your parents should be here by the time we've finished these tests, Trevor. Your neck is in a brace so you have limited movement but I need you to keep your body still too. If you can keep your eyes open please do, but if that is difficult then close and rest them as you need. I'll tell you what's happening but again we need you to remain very still. You are flat on a board on a stretcher, as you hit your head on something hard in the bus. You may have also hurt your neck and your back. We're about to take X-rays of your legs. I'll be stepping away for a moment and then I'll come right back. You're not alone.'

Jessica and the nurses stepped away momentarily while the radiologist took the images and then they all returned to find the boy's eyes wide open but staring straight ahead.

'You're doing so well, Trevor,' Jessica continued. 'I know I'm now upside down to you but I need to stand here at your head, so I can check your response to light. I will shine a small torch into your eyes; it won't hurt but I want you to keep looking at my nose.' The nurse handed Jessica the small torch and she shone it in sideways movements across Trevor's line of vision and then slowly in a circular motion. 'I'm going to cover one of your eyes and shine the light in the uncovered eye, then I will do the same to the other eye.'

Jessica completed the examination before turning to the nurse. 'The pupils are equal in size and responsive to light, which is a good sign, but the right eye is a little sluggish, which may be an issue. I just apologise that I don't know all of the consultants at the hospital; is there a neurologist on staff?'

'No, however, our ICU Consultant is on his way down now. A neurologist in Sydney was contacted by Dr Wainwright as his patient is suspected C1-C2 vertebrae damage. The neurologist is flying over tomorrow to assess the boy as he may need airlifting to the Sydney General Memorial Hospital for treatment.'

Jessica nodded her understanding of the situation in the adjacent bay and her appreciation of the ER team's initiative in sending for the ICU Consultant. She quickly returned her attention to her patient.

'You've been very good, Trevor,' Jessica told him and, casting a glance at the nurses' names, she turned back to him, adding, 'Nurse Jan and Nurse Gayle will stay with you and I will check back in a little while. If you have any questions, please ask them. And if you have any pain let them know. We're waiting for another special doctor to come and look at you and, in the meantime, I'm going to help one of your classmates who's been hurt too.'

Jessica discarded her gloves and rushed into the next bay, where an intern was attending another young victim. She had no idea where Harrison was but she could hear his voice and knew he was moving from one bay to the next, doing his best to keep each and every little patient alive.

It was going to be a long day and night for them all and Jessica hoped that no parent would be without their precious child by the end of it.

'Thank you,' Harrison said as he observed Jessica sign off on the last patient and release the young girl into the care of her very relieved and grateful parents.

His words were few but heartfelt. Jessica could see in his face that the pressure of the previous hours, constantly triaging patients and managing staff, had taken its toll. He was exhausted, mentally and physically.

'You don't need to thank me,' Jessica replied, pulling off her disposable surgical cap and gown, which was splattered with fine spots of her last patient's blood. The young girl had sustained lacerations to her forearm as fragments of plate glass window had cut through her sweater and lodged in her skin, but fortunately not compromised any blood supply. With one of the senior ER nurses assisting, Jessica had painstakingly removed the fine glass and stitched the wounds. It was one of the least serious injuries and, as such, had been left until last to ensure the patients with life-threatening injuries had been treated first.

It had been a long day and night for the ER team and the other medical staff called in from across the hospital as required. They had pulled together professionally and worked tirelessly to save the lives of all the children. While some of the injured students would spend an extended amount of time in hospital with their injuries, they had at least all pulled through. The less seriously injured patients would be transferred to the Tamworth General Hospital the following day to make it easier on family and friends visiting them, but at least two young boys would have to remain in Armidale for an indefinite period. They had not been wearing their seat belts and had, as a result, sustained neck and back injuries that required ongoing monitoring in the ICU as unnecessary travel would not be permitted.

'It's one a.m.,' Harrison commented in passing to the staff who had worked past the end of their shifts to treat the patients. 'Great job—please go home and if you're rostered on tomorrow, don't show up. We'll move staff around the hospital to cover for you. And if any of you usually catch public transport across the New England area, please get a cab and the hospital will reimburse you.'

All the staff thanked Harrison and left for the day. Weary but satisfied with the outcome of the horrific accident. They were all saddened to know the bus driver had lost his life but relieved that the children had not.

'How about you, Dr Ayers? Do you have transport?' Harrison asked Jessica as she made her way to leave.

'Yes,' she said as she turned to face him.

'But thank you for asking. I have my rental in the doctors' car park.'

'If you'd like to get your things from your office, I'm more than happy to walk you to your car. It's a bit isolated out the back, especially at this hour, and not particularly well lit in some places.'

Jessica nodded. 'Thank you; that's very kind of you.'

'It's settled then. I'll grab my jacket and meet you back here in ten minutes.'

Jessica returned to her office and collected her overcoat and handbag. On the way out she called in and caught up with the night staff in Paediatrics and was brought up to speed on her patients. Thankfully, there was nothing to report; all were progressing well with their treatment and Jessica told them she would be back for morning rounds. She returned to the ER to find Harrison waiting, just as he'd said he would. An unexpected warm feeling washed over her. It felt good to have someone looking out for her. She had been doing it alone for the best part of a year and it hadn't bothered her, but seeing Harrison there made her feel unexpectedly safe for the first time in a long time.

And she didn't want to run from that feeling.

'I can't believe how freezing cold it can get in this town. I don't think I've lived anywhere that drops down this low,' Jessica remarked as she dug her hands into the deep pockets of her heavy woollen coat. Her breath was fogging the still night air as she spoke.

'Heads up, Dr Ayers—one in the morning, slap bang in the middle of winter, isn't the best time to get out and about in many places around here!' Harrison laughed as they picked up speed and headed to the doctors' car park at the rear of the hospital. 'And if you didn't already know, Armidale has the highest altitude of any city in Australia.'

'So now I know why almost every house I drive past has a stockpile of wood. They know what they're in for in winter.'

'Yes, and nothing beats an open fire,' he returned, rubbing his hands together as if over the flames.

Jessica smiled and kept walking. The con-

versation was flowing and she felt at ease...
but that was almost making her uneasy.

'At least it's not raining and you don't have
far to drive,' Harrison continued.

'That's the joy of not being in a big city. You
can drive for what seems like hours in Sydney or Melbourne to get home after a long
shift, which isn't pleasant and the last thing
you need when all you want is to put your feet
up and collapse on the sofa because you have
an early start the next morning.'

'So, you're not a lover of big cities then?'

'I'm not averse to living in large cities. I
mean it has its advantages but there's the
downside too, and I don't have to deal with
that here, which is a bonus. I'll be home in
five minutes and that's a big plus—particularly at one in the morning, *slap-bang in the
middle of winter*!'

Another bonus was being walked to her car
by a handsome medical colleague and that
hadn't happened in any city placements, but
Jessica wasn't about to mention that to Harrison. She was still coming to terms with how
her feelings were developing for the man, no

matter how hard she fought to remind herself that men were not permitted within a mile of her or her heart. But the more she spent time with Harrison, the more difficult it became to ignore the respect she had for him as a doctor, a godfather and a colleague.

And a chivalrous man.

'So, is Armidale winning over the city girl?'

'I'm not sure,' she replied as she reached inside her handbag for her keys. 'I haven't been here long enough yet…but, from what I've seen of the town over the last few days, it's a lovely lifestyle and such a supportive community spirit.'

Harrison smiled and Jessica wasn't sure if the smile was pride in his home town or something else but she thought it best to leave it at that as she pressed on the small electronic remote key to unlock the drivers' door.

'Thank you, Harrison, for walking me to my car. I really do appreciate it.' The car park was dimly lit in places, just as Harrison had told her, and she had parked her small red hatchback in one of the darkest places.

'It's the least I can do when you just worked a sixteen-hour shift.'

'As did you, and all of the others. I don't deserve any more praise than everyone else.' With that she opened the door and climbed in the car, but not before saying goodnight.

Harrison bid her goodnight and she watched as he walked away to a better lit part of the car park. Cutting a powerful figure with his broad shoulders and long powerful steps, he crossed to a large black four-wheel drive. She couldn't help but stare as he climbed in. She wanted to pull her gaze away but she felt a strange connection to him. It didn't make sense but it was there. Jessica couldn't deny it, nor could she define it.

Within moments he started the car and headed to the exit. Quickly, Jessica was brought back to the task at hand. Getting home and not thinking about Dr Harrison Wainwright. He had walked her to her car, not rescued her from a burning house. She needed to put everything in perspective.

Romance in a rural city was not on the cards.

Romance anywhere was not on the cards. End of story.

Then why was she sitting in a dark car park thinking about it?

Quickly she checked her mobile phone for messages. There was nothing urgent so she slipped it inside her handbag on the seat beside her. It was a short drive so she kept her coat on, as she knew the car would barely warm up before she would be pulling up in her driveway. Ready to go, she turned on the ignition. There was nothing. She tried again, but again the engine didn't turn over at all. Nothing happened. She dropped her head on the steering wheel for a moment, realising in an instant that her rental had a flat battery. She wasn't going anywhere.

Harrison had left and she was in the darkest part of the deserted car park with no one in sight. Suddenly feeling safe flew out through the ice-covered window. She tried to pull her tired mind into action. She could run back inside and call a cab, but if Harrison had insisted on walking her to the car, maybe walking back on her own wasn't the best idea. Perhaps she could call roadside assistance, if there was any. It wasn't Sydney and she had no clue if the local provider would be on duty. And what was the number anyway?

Jessica unexpectedly felt a little close to tears. It had been a long day, an incredibly long day, and all she wanted was a nice warm bed for the next six hours. She'd been so relieved that the patients had all survived but managing that stress had taken its toll on her emotional reserves. And now, when she needed sleep almost as much as air, she wasn't sure when she would get to bed. Not to mention the fact that being in the darkness of the car park was starting to add to her angst. She reached down to the glovebox to see if there was any information about who to call in case of a breakdown.

Suddenly there was a tap on the car window.

Jessica screamed and jumped as she turned to see a tall outline standing beside the car door. A towering figure that made her feel more vulnerable by the second and made her heart pick up speed. Her body was instantly in fight or flight mode. She realised this was probably why Harrison had insisted on walking her to the car.

The tapping continued until a mobile phone illuminated the stranger's face.

Only it wasn't a stranger.

'Oh, my God, Harrison!' she exclaimed as she opened the door a little, her hand still visibly shaking and her heart still racing. 'What are you doing here? I thought you'd left—I saw you drive off.'

'I did, but I didn't see your lights in my rear mirror as I turned onto the road so I came back. I thought there might be something wrong. Am I right or did I just scare the living daylights out of you for no good reason?'

'No, you're right,' she said with a rueful half smile. 'I'm guessing I have a flat battery. There's nothing when I turn on the ignition,' she continued, then took a deep breath, encouraging her heart to slow down.

'I suspected car trouble. I didn't think you'd choose to sit in the middle of a deserted car park in the early hours to check your social media,' he said, smiling.

'Not usually.' Her eyes rolled but the smile remained.

'So your car is effectively dead at the moment and, as I don't have any leads to jumpstart your battery, we have two options. We call for roadside assistance and hope they're not caught up elsewhere, which may well be the case as there's not too many service providers after hours, or I drop you home and collect you again in the morning from your home and we call roadside assistance to replace the battery then.'

Jessica nodded. 'Option two sounds much better, if you're sure you don't mind?'

'I don't mind at all. In fact, if you'd chosen option one I would've tried to talk you into option two, just to save my fingers from frostbite.'

Ten minutes later they arrived at Jessica's home. All the houses were in darkness and Harrison insisted on walking Jessica to the door.

'I'm going to make a hot chocolate before I turn in for the night,' she said as she felt around in her bag for her keys. 'I can just as easily make two, if you would like one?'

She froze as the words slipped from her lips. It scared her that it seemed so natural to ask him in.

Her mind-set on the day she'd arrived couldn't have been further from where it was at that moment. Harrison was like no one she had met before and, while part of her felt she needed her barriers up perhaps even more than usual, there was another part that felt comfortable and relaxed in his presence and, despite the late hour, something was pushing her to spend some time alone to get to know the man who had been so gallant on more than one occasion. He seemed genuinely nice, he was an amazing doctor under pressure and…she silently admitted that, against her better judgement, she was very curious to learn more. It was that simple and nothing about her life had been simple for a very long time.

Harrison hesitated then turned and remotely locked his car.

'I'd like that, but I'm only staying for ten minutes; you need your sleep.'

'And you need yours too,' Jessica replied as she opened the front door and invited him in.

An hour later Harrison stood to leave, not because he wanted to go but because he knew he should. While Bryce was with his grandparents for the night, as he often was when Harrison was working, he wanted to have breakfast with his son the way he always did. Whether they were in their own home or with Harrison's parents, sharing breakfast was a ritual he didn't break often or without good reason. The trip to LA recently had meant they'd missed six shared breakfasts and Harrison didn't want to miss another one.

It was after two in the morning and ten minutes had turned into sixty. Hot chocolate had been accompanied by crumpets with honey and he couldn't remember feeling so comfortable outside his own home. Jessica was sitting on the sofa with him, her legs curled up underneath her. She had excused herself and quickly changed into sweat pants and an oversized jumper while the crumpets were cooking. And, while there was no roaring fire, the central heating had kept them both warm. And the conversation had found Harrison warming to Jessica by the minute and opening up about certain aspects of his life. Each had spoken about their respective journeys to becoming doctors, their reasons for choosing medicine and their experiences on the job, good and bad, including how they dealt with telling the families they had lost their loved one. Both agreed this was the hardest part of their work.

And both had skilfully and purposely avoided the topic of relationships. Jessica hadn't asked about Harrison's past, nor he about hers. It definitely made the evening even more pleasant for him and he suspected perhaps for her too. Bringing Bryce's mother into the conversation would have spoilt everything and brought him back to earth with a thud. And it was too early to mention his son. While Jessica was lovely, unless a miracle happened, she was only in town for a short time and he felt protective of Bryce. There was no need to bring him up yet. Or perhaps ever.

Despite being exhausted, he really didn't want to leave but knew he should for Jessica's sake. 'I've kept you up far too long, and if I don't go now I risk falling asleep on the sofa, not a good look for the neighbours,' he said as he stacked the cups and plates, ready to take them to the kitchen.

He couldn't help but notice Jessica smile a little sheepishly, he assumed at the thought of him staying over. He was suddenly further drawn towards the gorgeous paediatrician who had waltzed into town and made him question much about his life. The idea of staying over was definitely very appealing. She was a stunning conundrum. She had spent the last sixteen hours showing her extraordinary abilities and dedication as a doctor; she was not timid in voicing her opinions; she had a wonderful way of making him feel at ease without trying; and she was gorgeous. Without knowing it, Dr Jessica Ayers was making Harrison question his resolve to only date women who had no further appeal than a great night of sex with no strings attached. He suspected Jessica would come with strings and, for some reason, he wasn't running away. But *she* would be soon enough. She hadn't hidden that fact, yet, despite it, he still didn't want to go.

In fact, it was just the opposite; he was forcing himself to leave. The thought of strings was not a barrier to spending time with her. It was as if he was open to becoming a little entangled, for however long that might be. He would just make sure that it wouldn't involve Bryce. Harrison's personal life would always be kept very separate to his family life.

Together they walked to the kitchen and put everything in the sink. Jessica told him she would wash them in the morning.

'Thank you again for bringing me home,' Jessica said as she followed Harrison to the front door.

'And don't forget to thank me for almost scaring you to death in the car park.'

Jessica laughed. 'It *was* a little horror movie-esque.'

'I promise not to sneak up like that again...'

'Let's hope my car doesn't break down again.'

Jessica reached up and took Harrison's jacket from the wall-mounted coat rail. His hand brushed against hers as he took it from her but, instead of slipping it on, he paused for a moment so close to her. He didn't want to leave. He knew at that moment he wanted more than anything to taste the sweetness of her lips. To pull her body against his and hold her in his arms. It all seemed so natural. There was no doubt, no questions. He didn't need to second-guess. His lips were hovering only inches from the inviting softness of her mouth. The mouth he wanted more than anything to claim, the mouth that suddenly...

Yawned.

Harrison stepped back. 'Oh...that would be my cue to go...'

'Oh, my God, I'm so sorry,' she said and, covering her mouth with her hand, yawned for a second time. 'It's not you...it's just...'

'It's just that you've worked a day from hell and I've kept you up talking for another hour and I almost...' Harrison stopped mid-sentence, raking his hair. He didn't want to admit he had almost kissed her. She knew— they both knew what had almost happened—

but he suspected the moment had passed. 'I've almost outstayed my welcome.'

Harrison watched as Jessica's gaze fell to her slippers and then came back to him again. Her eyes were wide and she was smiling, albeit a little embarrassed, just as she had looked at their airport encounter.

'You haven't at all. I've really enjoyed getting to know you.' Her voice was so low that he almost missed what she had said. 'Truly, I've enjoyed spending time with you.'

'I've enjoyed it too,' Harrison said, unsure of many things but realising, yawn or no yawn, he still wanted to kiss her more than he could remember wanting anything. He wasn't going to second-guess himself.

Gently he pulled her close to him and, as his mouth moved towards hers, she tilted her face to him and closed her eyes in anticipation. Their lips met with a tenderness and an almost wonderful familiarity that lovers shared. Such closeness didn't make sense to him, but nothing since meeting Jessica had. She pressed her body against his and his arms held her even more tightly. He didn't want it to end.

Swept away by the feelings surging through his body, Harrison wanted to hold her in his arms and feel the warmth of her mouth on his for the longest time. It was a gentle release of feelings, not wildly passionate. Harrison was holding back because he sensed, for reasons he did not yet know, that Jessica needed him to go slowly with her.

Suddenly he felt her stiffen in his arms.

His arm slowly released his embrace as he stepped back and looked at the most beautiful woman he had ever seen. Looking in her eyes, he could see something that wasn't fear but it was close to it. His instincts had been correct.

'Is everything all right?' he asked as he collected himself.

'Yes, it's just that…we should get some sleep,' she said tentatively. 'You need to drive home and we'll have a big day tomorrow, I'm sure, with all the patients to be discharged or transferred to Tamworth.'

Harrison wasn't sure what had happened and why Jessica was pulling away, but he did as he was asked. He wasn't about to press her to find out. Perhaps she was right in pulling away; while he had enjoyed spending time with Jessica, he had not imagined when he drove her home that he would lose perspective and so quickly overstep the boundaries. She was a work colleague and Harrison had, until now, always kept his private life away from the hospital. The entire evening, even wanting to stay for a warm drink in the first place, went against his better judgement. But he had done it anyway. It was obvious to him that there was chemistry between them, but as her actions made him step back he was reminded that what he'd done went against everything he believed. Jessica was only in town for a limited time.

Again, he needed to remind himself, his ex-wife had been in town for a limited time too. The situation screamed déjà-vu and Harrison could not afford to relive that nightmare. He couldn't allow his emotions to get the better of him. He had made that mistake before. Allowed himself to be swept away, falling heart and soul way too soon and then being helpless to prevent it all falling apart. He couldn't travel that road again, but would it be the same road? he wondered. Or was this very different? Harrison's head was telling him to pull back but his heart was saying something very different.

They were two professional people who had spent time getting to know each other outside of work and he had allowed it to go too far. Now he needed to take her cue and set boundaries. Jessica had been upfront about her intentions. Stay six weeks and leave town. There had been no deceit, no false promises. He had to try and colleague zone Jessica immediately and put some distance between them. He had no choice, for his own sake. But he doubted how successful it would be after the kiss they'd shared.

'I'll send a cab for you in the morning at about ten-thirty, if that suits you?'

'A cab?'

'Yes, you deserve a decent sleep, so you can start late. I'll head in earlier and check on our patients before they're transported to Tamworth.'

'I can assist with that…'

'You've done enough.' Enough to unsettle

him. Enough to even at that moment make him want to pull her close again. Enough to make him kiss her again. He was so confused, and she had made him think clearly when he'd felt her pull away. Now he had to do it too. 'I'll email hospital admin when I get home and let them know to roster cover for you until eleven. It's not the entire day off, but it's a few extra hours' sleep. I arranged the same for the other staff before I left. And the neurosurgeon is flying in from Sydney mid-morning, to consult on the two suspected spinal cord injury patients.'

'You certainly have everything under control.'

'It's best for everyone that way.' Though Harrison knew he was losing control with Jessica. And that was not the best option for a man who had finally gained control of his life.

His tone had changed and he could see it hadn't gone unnoticed by Jessica. *Torn* best described how he felt. He didn't understand what he had seen in her eyes only moments before. It confused him. Her gorgeously messy blonde hair fell around her beautiful face and

she looked less like an accomplished temporary Paediatric Consultant from a large city
hospital and more like a fresh-faced country
girl. She was so close he could reach out and
cup her beautiful face in his hands and kiss
her again.

He had to leave before he went mad with the
gamut of emotions he was feeling.

Opening the door, he walked into the icy
night air without stopping to put on his jacket.

Or saying goodnight.

CHAPTER SEVEN

JESSICA LAY IN BED, staring in the darkness at the ceiling, wondering what on earth had happened. And as she rolled onto her side again and curled her legs up under the warmth of the heavy woollen blankets, she wondered what could have happened if she hadn't pulled away. Gently her fingers pressed against her mouth and for a moment she relived the tenderness of his kiss. A kiss she hadn't imagined would ever happen until just before it did.

Standing so close, when he'd looked into her eyes, her body had rendered her helpless to think logically. To think that she should say no, move away and not give into her feelings. But instead she had surrendered to them. It concerned her that increasingly she was losing perspective and presence of mind around him.

Sleep evaded her for close to an hour, as

nothing about her bed was comfortable that night. She tossed and turned all the while, questioning why she'd pushed away every promise she had made to herself about getting close to a man again. She had invited him in for a hot chocolate. And then gave him crumpets. What had she been thinking? And what had he been thinking to accept? And as he'd leant in towards her, she'd known he was going to kiss her. And she'd welcomed the kiss. What if he had wanted to stay longer? What would have happened? Would they have given in to their mutual desire? Or would they have come to their senses? So many questions and absolutely no certainty in the answers swirling about inside Jessica's head.

But one thing was for sure—nothing about the placement was going as planned. Not from the get-go with the lost luggage and then the dressing-down by Harrison. And why on earth would she be interested in a man who turned hot and cold like that? Jessica knew the answer. Because Harrison was like no one she had met before. He was a great doctor, a wonderful leader, an amazingly supportive friend to those who needed him most and…and now she knew he was capable of giving the most amazing kiss. The thought of it made her heart beat a little faster than it should.

She knew for certain that she must have gone mad as she rolled back onto her side, pulled the covers up around her ears and finally succumbed to a restless slumber. Dreams of Harrison's handsome chiselled face so close to hers…dreams of that fateful phone call from the woman whose cheating husband had been her lover…and finally dreams of drowning in a tidal wave that washed over Armidale but claimed only her.

Harrison woke early, showered and drove over to his parents' home to have breakfast at eight o'clock. He had managed to get five hours' sleep but, whether awake or drifting off to sleep, his mind was filled with thoughts of Jessica and the kiss they'd shared the night before…how good it felt to have her in his arms.

While wondering if perhaps everything was moving too fast, he strongly doubted he could put the brakes on it now. And he wasn't sure if he would if he could.

'Daddy!'

Harrison scooped up the excited five-year-old in his arms and whizzed him around the huge country-style kitchen.

'Be careful,' Harrison's mother, Anthea, said sternly. 'You might break something.'

Harrison kissed the top of Bryce's head before he put him back down. 'We'd better listen to Granny or we'll both be in trouble.'

'That you will. I learnt that about forty years ago,' came a voice from the adjacent sun room.

'Morning, Dad.'

'Morning, Harrison,' his father said as he made his way into the kitchen, popped his newspaper on the bench, pulled out one of the oak chairs and sat down.

'How was Bryce last night? Did he behave and go to bed on time without any protest?'

'An angel, as always,' Anthea cut in, not waiting for her husband to answer as she put a stack of freshly made waffles on the table. There was already butter, jam and cream to be dolloped on the waffles, along with a plate of fresh fruit. She looked at Harrison and Bryce and continued, 'Please, sit down, Harrison, and eat up while I get showered and dressed.'

Harrison sat down and looked over the breakfast spread. 'It's amazing, Mum, but honestly oatmeal would have been enough. You do too much.'

'Don't be ridiculous, Harrison. Bryce loves Granny's waffles. Don't you?' she asked, looking at the little boy.

'I love them!' Bryce answered as he reached for one of the golden-brown breakfast treats.

'Clearly my time spent cooking was justified.' With that, Anthea untied her apron, draped it over an empty chair at the kitchen table and exited the room.

Harrison and his father, David, both shook their heads. There was no point arguing with a doting grandmother.

'So, everything went okay last night?' Harrison asked as he reached for a waffle too. He passed on the jam and cream, instead layering slices of the fresh fruit. He rarely ate an unhealthy breakfast but he didn't want to hurt his mother's feelings and decline the waffle.

'Why do you ask?'

'I just want to know you're okay with it. I mean, if it gets too much having Bryce over-night, let me know.' Harrison's voice was lowered and Bryce was concentrating on the cartoons he could see on the television in the other room and paying little attention to the adult conversation.

'As if he would ever be too much,' David scoffed.

'He'll be back again tonight because of the hospital fund-raising gala at the Art Museum and I don't want you missing out on sleep.'

'We absolutely love having him over and we're looking forward to having him again tonight, even if I lose every game of Go Fish. But he did complain a little about a pain in his tummy before he went to bed. Although he seems fine this morning so it's probably nothing.'

Harrison turned immediately to face his son and bring him back in the chat. 'How are you feeling now, Bryce? Grandpa said you had a tummy ache last night.'

'I did but my tummy doesn't hurt now,' he

replied as he spread strawberry jam on a second waffle and turned his attention back to the cartoons.

Harrison looked over at his father. 'By his appetite, I'd say he's okay but I'll take a look at him tonight. Please call me if the stomach ache comes back. It might be a bit of residual anxiety from me being away,' Harrison said, looking from his son and then to his watch before standing and taking his plate to the sink. 'I'd better head in; we had multiple injuries from a bus accident late yesterday and a few are transferring to Tamworth today.'

'Are you going, Daddy?' Bryce asked.

'Yes, I need to go into the hospital. Granny's taking you to school.'

'Will you pick me up?' the little boy continued with an expectant look on his face, his big blue eyes the exact hue of his father's.

'Yes.'

'Yippee.'

'And we'll have a few hours together then I'll need to head out to a party tonight for the hospital, so you will spend another night with Granny and Grandpa.'

'Are you going to a birthday party? Will there be a clown and cake and stuff? Can I come too?'

Harrison smiled. 'No, there won't be cake or clowns and there definitely won't be a bouncy castle. This is a special party where we will talk a lot and raise money to help the hospital to buy new machines to keep people healthy, so I think it would be more fun for you with Granny and Grandpa.'

Bryce tilted his head on one side. 'Okay.'

'But I need you to tell Granny or Grandpa if your tummy starts to hurt again.'

'Okay.'

Harrison kissed his son, put his dishes in the dishwasher and bid farewell to his father. 'I'm sure he's okay but please just keep an eye on him this evening.'

'Will do.'

Jessica arrived in time to check in on the last three patients still waiting to be transported to their home town. They had improved overnight and she felt confident that after their transfer all three would be released from Tam-

worth Hospital within days. The two most seriously injured boys, one of whom had the
suspected spinal cord injury, had been admitted to Armidale Regional Memorial, along
with four other children whose families pre-
ferred that they remained in Armidale until
they were well enough to be released. They either worked or had family in the town so pre-
ferred the children didn't leave hospital until
they were completely healed.

Jessica couldn't see Harrison anywhere,
which suited her. It had ended awkwardly the
night before and, despite a restless night and
mixed feelings, she wondered on the short
drive to the hospital whether the yawn had
been a sign from the universe that the kiss
should never have happened. But it had, and
she wondered if it would or could stop there.
With that thought firmly in her mind, no clue
where Harrison was and a decision to keep
her distance until she knew how she felt, she
headed up to ICU to check on the two boys'
progress.

'I can see their vitals are stable. How did
they go with pain during the night?' Jessica

asked the ICU nurse attending to the boys. The hospital had eleven specialist departments but these did not include a Spinal Injuries Unit so the young patients had been transferred to the Intensive Care Unit rather than Paediatrics. Their injuries were still critical and the monitoring requirements were more aligned to ICU.

'Stable, nothing to worry us during the night,' the nurse replied as she checked the intravenous fluid flow on the patient with the head injury and fractured legs. 'They're on IV pain relief and Dr Jeffries, the neurosurgeon, should arrive here from Sydney within the hour.'

'So still no feeling or movement in the limbs of the C1-C2 vertebrae injured patient?'

The nurse shook her head.

Jessica nodded knowingly but said nothing. It was not going to be an easy road ahead for the young boy or his family if the damage was permanent. Jessica was relieved that the neurosurgeon was on his way. He would at least provide clarity for the family on the next steps.

She returned to Paediatrics and checked in on her patients, all of whom were progressing well and there were thankfully no changes. Four of the children from the bus accident had been admitted and she intended on keeping them for one more day. Suddenly she realised it was Friday and, while she would stay on until late that night, she wasn't rostered on over the weekend. She was on call for emergencies but not physically in the hospital. What was there for her to do in country New South Wales on a weekend? she wondered.

The movies? Dinner? Or stay in and watch cable television? All sounded fine to her, as did sleeping in again for two days. It had been a very busy week and the night before had been exhausting and then confusing so she was relieved that she would have two days to do whatever she wanted and potentially nothing.

'Dr Ayers,' Rosie called as Jessica walked past the administration desk.

'Yes, Rosie?'

'Are you going to the hospital fund-raiser tonight?'

'No, I haven't heard anything about a fund-raiser.'

'I thought you might not know,' the nurse replied, walking out from behind the desk. 'It's quite a swanky affair at the NERAM. It's to raise funds for the Renal Dialysis Unit. A very worthwhile cause.'

'The NERAM?'

'The New England Region Art Museum; it's lovely and not far from here. Five minutes and loads of parking.'

Jessica smiled and nodded. Rosie was doing her best sales pitch and that didn't go unnoticed by Jessica. 'It certainly is a very worthwhile cause but I didn't start work until almost eleven this morning so I'm not about to leave early to attend an event, besides which I don't have a ticket.'

'The ticket's not a problem. I'm on the social committee and there's still a few remaining tickets so, if you can get the evening off, then I can arrange a ticket.'

'I don't think so. I should be here at the hospital as I'm sure a lot of the hospital staff will be at the event.'

'As they will, my dear, and you're one of them,' a male voice told her.

Jessica turned to see Professor Langridge standing behind her, waving an envelope in his hand. 'Your ticket for tonight's shindig. I should have given this to you on your first day. My apologies. My wife reprimanded me for not giving it to you before now, so you had advance notice. It's apparently a woman thing, to plan what you're going to wear.'

'Professor, its lovely to see you but I really can't take time off. I've only been here for a couple of hours…'

'And a sixteen-hour day yesterday,' he countered. 'I don't know how hard they work you in the big cities, but in this town you get time off after a day like that. We like to keep our doctors alive and well and it's important that you have a work life balance here. Besides, I'd like you to come along and get to meet the other staff you haven't managed to catch up with yet.'

'Oh, I don't know, and to be honest I'm not sure I've brought anything suitable to wear to a charity fund-raiser.'

'Dr Ayers, it's a country fund-raiser; we've got no Royal family members coming along,'

Rosie piped up with a smile. 'So, nothing too formal—just a nice dress or suit would be fine.'

Just not jeans and runners, Jessica thought to herself, while acknowledging that no one had so much as muttered a word about her inappropriate clothes. They all really had accepted her as she arrived with no questions asked. The judgement was all hers. She wondered if that extended to other parts of her life. Was she perhaps her own harshest critic? She wasn't sure but she was beginning to think she should relax a little more and just enjoy the country life while she was there.

'Then it's set,' the Professor remarked as he put the envelope on the desk, tapping her name in bold print on the front with his fingers. 'I'll see you there tonight. You can meet my lovely wife and it'll be a good chance to mingle out of scrubs…and, oh, I can arrange a second ticket if you'd like to bring someone.'

Jessica surrendered on the spot. There was no point fighting both of them. She was attending the fund-raiser; that had been settled.

'Thank you, Errol. One ticket is enough. I don't have anyone to bring.'

* * *

Jessica worked until a quarter past six. The fund-raiser wasn't until seven-thirty and she wasn't going to be held up in either traffic leaving work or driving to the event at the Museum, only five minutes from home. The convenience of living in the town was starting to grow on Jessica. There was no horrible commute, an extremely friendly bunch of work colleagues and genuine community spirit and, apart from the fleeting belief she was being car-jacked the night before, she felt very safe.

She was glad she hadn't bumped into Harrison all day. It suited her because what had happened worried her.

The kiss had changed everything. It had changed how she felt about getting that close to someone…or where it might lead. He was a single, eligible doctor but was she ready to take it further? She couldn't have been more confused.

Arriving home, she turned on the central heating and made herself a cup of tea and a piece of toast topped with tomato and cheese.

Quite often with cocktail parties, the food, while delicious, was difficult to manage along with multiple conversations so she wanted something in her stomach. Jessica wasn't a big drinker but even one glass of wine on an empty stomach never ended well.

With a plate of comfort food in one hand and her cup of tea in the other, she made her way into her bedroom to select a suitable outfit for the event. She had unpacked her suitcase the morning after her first shift and, with everything now hanging in plain sight, she was grateful to see that she had brought her little black winter dress. It was fine wool, with a high collar, long sleeves and skimmed her knees. And being such a quality fabric, it wasn't creased. She found a pair of high black patent court shoes, a small clutch bag and sheer black hosiery. And the look was definitely not flirtatious. Quite the opposite. If there was a name for the style it would be *chic convent*.

With everything laid out on her bed, Jessica stepped into a steaming shower. It felt good to have the hot water wash over her and she silently admitted that a warm sofa and a good movie would have been her perfect evening and given her time to process what had happened the night before but, thanks to Errol and Rosie, she was not to be a master of her own destiny that night.

'It's great that you could make it,' Errol Langridge commented as he met Jessica entering the room, already buzzing with people and conversations. She had dropped her large caramel-coloured winter overcoat at the coat check at the entrance to the Art Museum.

'It was a bit of a surprise but I'm so glad to be here and it's such a worthwhile cause.' As Jessica looked around the museum, which was brimming with artefacts, she realised that it was far better being there than alone at home with a movie. She had plenty of time to do solo nights when she left Armidale.

'And please let me introduce you to my wife. Jessica, this is Grace…and Grace, darling, this is Dr Jessica Ayers, our locum paediatrician who, by all accounts, and I do mean all accounts, is doing a wonderful job.'

'Pleased to meet you,' Jessica said, extending her hand to Grace Langridge. She guessed the pretty woman to be in her early sixties; she had short blonde hair and was wearing an elegant navy dress that skimmed her knees. A single strand of freshwater pearls adorned her neck and she wore matching earrings.

'Lovely to meet you too, Jessica,' Grace replied.

'And thank you, Errol. I'm thoroughly enjoying my time here; you have such amazing staff and facilities and the final selling point of this placement is the drive to work every day; it's a dream,' Jessica laughed.

'Talking about placements, I thought I should warn you, young lady, we may try to keep you on staff. And there's more than one of your colleagues who would like to see that happen,' the Professor remarked as he took a glass of champagne from the tray being circulated by smartly dressed hospitality staff and handed it to his wife. 'Would you like some champagne, Jessica?'

Jessica nodded and Errol handed her a long-stemmed glass of bubbles, complete with a strawberry dressing the rim.

'Speaking of your fan club, Dr Ayers, the unabashed leader of it just arrived.'

Jessica turned around to see Harrison in the doorway. He took her breath away in his charcoal-grey suit, crisp white shirt and dark patterned tie. And perfect wide smile as he acknowledged one by one people he knew in the room.

He was the leader of her fan club?

She turned back, hoping she wasn't too obviously flushed. She could feel her cheeks warming and she hoped he continued to greet everyone individually, giving her cheeks time to calm down.

'Champagne does turn my cheeks rosy,' she mumbled to Grace and smiled a strained half smile.

'I can't see it, my dear, but then at your age a rosy glow would only make you look even more beautiful. I remember back to being as young as you when I met Errol.'

'Are you from the Armidale New England region or did you both move here?'

'Errol is actually from Uralla, a little town not far from here. He studied medicine in Sydney and returned to Armidale Regional Memorial as an intern a long time ago. I was in my third year of practice at a leading physiotherapy clinic in Melbourne. Goodness, I loved it and planned on opening my own clinic by the time I reached thirty. I was a city girl with city dreams and then I met a country boy when I was having an evening out with some girlfriends. Errol was in town for a conference. In one night he turned my life completely upside down. In a matter of weeks, I literally gave up everything and moved here.'

'Wow. That is quite a whirlwind romance. I thought that only happened in movies and books.' Jessica was taken aback by Grace's story.

'Yes, it was a wow moment.' She dropped her voice a little, took a sip of her champagne and added, 'My friends and family thought I was completely mad and I must admit I had a few misgivings myself along the way, particularly in the lead up to the move, but once I settled in I couldn't imagine my life anywhere else. I'm truly blessed, Jessica, to have met Errol. He's my soulmate.'

'Well, you certainly took a huge risk and I'm so happy that it worked out so wonderfully for you. I couldn't leave everything for a man I barely knew.'

Grace patted her hand. 'You would for the right man.'

'Ah, Harrison, so good to see you here,' Errol announced as he took a glass of red wine from the waiter circulating with a tray of red and white wines then whispered to Jessica, 'I was wondering when the good stuff would come out; I'm not a bubbles and strawberries kind of man.'

Jessica smiled at Errol's remark but her mind was elsewhere. She suddenly wished she was at home on the sofa with a movie and didn't have to face her own feelings. Feelings that were confusing and scaring her in equal amounts. And all of them about Harrison.

Harrison approached the trio and greeted Errol with a firm handshake, then Grace with an endearing kiss on the cheek. Jessica's stomach did a somersault, wondering how he would greet her. She shifted anxiously on her stilettos and took a gulp of her champagne. Would it be a colleague's handshake, a nod or…? Suddenly her answer came as he stepped forward and gently kissed her on the cheek. A tender kiss that allowed her to feel the softness of his skin as it brushed against hers and for the freshness of his woody cologne to fill her senses. Making her body feel alive with little effort. Just as he had the night before.

'Hello, Jessica.'

'Hello, Harrison.'

Time disappeared for the briefest moment as he stepped back and their eyes locked. The room was empty except for them. She could feel her heart beating and felt herself struggling to breathe. She had to pull herself back from falling into something that scared her to the core so she hurriedly took another sip of her champagne.

'You look gorgeous, Jessica, as do you, Grace.'

'I know,' Errol cut in before the ladies could respond. 'We've certainly got the finest fillies in the room.'

Grace gave a delicate laugh. 'No amount of time spent visiting my family or his many, many years studying in Sydney will take the country boy out of my husband.'

'And would you really want that, darling?'

'Not in a million years.'

Jessica watched as Errol lifted his wife's hand in his, tenderly kissing it as he looked into her eyes. 'And I would not change anything about you, my city born and bred wife either.'

'Would you like to try some kangaroo and salt bush canapés?' a young waiter interrupted as he held out a platter of the tasty delicacies.

'Sounds delicious,' Grace said as she reached for one, as did her husband. 'I've not tried salt bush.'

Harrison looked over at Jessica and again she felt her pulse quickening. 'I'm game to try something new tonight, if you are, Jessica?'

The blue of his eyes seemed to be sparkling even more brightly and she felt drawn in like a moth to a light.

'I've eaten native bush food quite a bit. There's a stall in the market not far from one of the hospitals where I had a placement four months ago and the Indigenous owners have tastings of different herbs and meat. They also tell you how to prepare them at home.' Jessica reached for one of the tiny wafers, dressed with a thin roll of kangaroo and a sprig of salt bush. She took a bite, knowing she would love the salty tang of the greenery and the depth of flavour of the kangaroo.

She watched as Harrison downed the small cracker in one mouthful and waited for his reaction, wondering if he would enjoy it as much as she had.

'That was amazing. Would it be rude to ask for a second?' Harrison enquired of the waiter still hovering near them.

'Not at all. That's why I always wait,' the man said with a smile. 'Because everyone wants more of these.'

The four all accepted the young man's offer and each reached for a second, before Errol and Grace excused themselves to mingle with the other guests, leaving Harrison and Jessica alone.

'You constantly surprise me,' Harrison remarked as he leant against the wall with his glass of red wine.

Jessica dabbed her mouth with a cocktail napkin before taking the final sip of her drink. While she always had a two-drink limit for an entire night, her Dutch courage suddenly needed refilling and her eyes searched the room for a waitress with white wine or something bubbly. 'How so?'

'A city girl who likes bush tucker and knows how to cook it. That's a skill not many would have, whether living in the city or the country. I wouldn't have a clue how to prepare food of Indigenous origins. Maybe I could throw a crocodile sausage on the grill but that would be my limit.'

Jessica laughed. 'I guess deep down I'm pretty much a homebody who loves cooking and it's not very difficult if you are taught by people who have worked with this food for a long time,' she said, trying to mask her borderline nervousness being around him. She found it hard to forget that in the early hours of that day they had kissed. And, more importantly, why they had kissed.

And why, if left alone, they might again.

Harrison broke into her thoughts. 'There's a lot of layers to you, Jessica.'

'I'm not that complex really,' she replied, grateful that he couldn't read her mind or feel her pulse as it was racing.

'I disagree, but how about I get you another champagne and, before the auction begins, show you around the museum, introduce you to some of the hospital staff you may not have met, and enlighten you to some local New England history in an attempt to impress you?'

Jessica found it so strange that Harrison was apparently oblivious to the fact that he had impressed her many times since their first accidental meeting.

Probably most of all when he'd pulled her close and kissed her.

Willingly she allowed him to escort her around the Art Museum and they stopped to greet some of the staff and their respective partners along the way. Harrison soon proved with little effort that he knew a great deal about the artworks and the history of the region. Jessica was at once enjoying her time with Harrison and quickly found herself less and less self-conscious in his presence. Their banter was light and easy and occasionally she felt his hand in the middle of her back as he guided her through the small groups to another piece of artwork. She leant into it and enjoyed the feeling. It made her feel as if she had someone taking care of her, if only for a short while, and it felt good. His attentiveness wasn't forced. Nor was her appreciation of him.

The auction, and the reason they had all come together, finally began. Harrison bid for the third item, a four-night Sydney getaway at one of the finest hotels with flights included, that had been generously donated by the local travel agent. Jessica watched on keenly as the ten bidders were knocked out one by one. Finally, there were two left and Harrison was the one with the leading bid.

'I'm bid ten thousand dollars,' the auctioneer announced. 'Does anyone care to raise that?'

'Ten thousand five hundred,' the other bidder announced with a confident tone. Jessica could see it was all done in good fun, for a good cause, but there was some old-fashioned male rivalry helping to get the bids up.

'Fifteen thousand,' Harrison announced. 'Just so we can get on with the next item.'

The crowd laughed, including the other bidder. 'Fair call,' he said. 'It has been dragging on a bit. It's all yours, Harrison. I'm out.'

The auctioneer called the bid and announced Harrison the winner. He approached the administrator for the night and gave him his credit card details to pay for the item. Then he returned to Jessica and slipped the envelope inside his suit jacket. 'Since I don't know anyone in Sydney, and you know it very well, I might be calling on you to show me around.'

Jessica was speechless. Had he bid an extraordinary amount just to spend time with her? The way he was looking at her, she very much suspected that was the case. Perhaps the kiss they'd shared did mean something more to him.

Jessica wasn't sure about anything except she was growing closer to the man standing next to her by the minute. He was everything she was not looking for when she'd flown into Armidale...but now she felt he was everything she knew she wanted.

'It's only eight-thirty, so not overly late, and I was wondering if you might like to go back to my house and chat some more without that auctioneer's voice drowning us out?'

Jessica drew breath. Her heart was racing at a ridiculous pace. She couldn't think of anything better...or riskier than being alone with Harrison. And that excited her.

'Let's claim our overcoats and exit. Is your car outside?'

'Yes.'

'If you're happy to follow me in your car, my home is literally walking distance from here.'

Harrison's home was, as he'd said, only three minutes from the Art Museum. It was a large two-storey redbrick home with a sweeping return driveway and beautifully manicured gardens. Jessica was taken aback by the size and grandeur. As she'd not yet driven past that part of the town, she had not seen it before. Harrison pulled his car into the large double garage and walked over to Jessica as she alighted from her car in front of the porch, where she saw an old-style wicker set including a double swing.

It was picture-postcard-perfect and so was Harrison.

'Let's get you inside where it's warmer than out here,' he said, taking her hand, and she felt certain that he intended to take things further than simply repaying her hospitality. She wasn't sure but, with her heart beating so fast, this time she had no intention of pulling away. This time she wanted to forget the past.

She wanted to live in the moment and throw everything else, including logic, out of her mind.

Harrison knew where he wanted to take the evening. He had grown close to Jessica very quickly but his feelings were real. And by the way she was reacting to him, he suspected she felt the same way. He hoped that the night would grow into something more. Suddenly and without reservation he wanted and felt ready to open his heart and his life to the mysterious woman who had arrived without warning. And very soon he planned that Bryce would meet the most amazing woman Harrison had ever laid eyes upon.

He turned on the dim lights and, without hesitation, lifted Jessica's hand to his lips and kissed the inside of her wrist. She was trembling just a little with anticipation, not fear. Tenderly his fingers traced the soft line of her jaw until he reached her chin. Purposefully, he lifted her face to his and his eyes told her everything she needed to know. He wanted her as much as she wanted him.

'I want more than anything to kiss you again. You must know that.'

Jessica nodded and lifted her face towards him. His mouth met hers this time with an urgency she had never felt in any man's kiss before. She met his passion and made it clear that not only her mouth was wanting to be claimed. She was his for the night.

'Are you sure, absolutely sure?' His voice

was low and the look in his eyes was piercing her soul.

Jessica nodded and breathlessly she told him, 'Yes.'

'No second thoughts?'

'None.'

Harrison wasn't going to ask again. He didn't need further confirmation that he was not alone in his desire to spend the night together. He didn't need any more encouragement to take her. To make her his own.

He bent his knees slightly to reach around her body and lift her into his embrace. His lips searched for hers again and he hoped the fire in his kiss told Jessica how he was feeling as he carried her into his bedroom then softly but purposely kicked the door closed behind them. This night was for the two of them and nothing and no one was going to take that away from them. No one was going to make him turn away from the most desirable woman he had ever met in his life.

There were many hours until the sun rose and Harrison intended to make use of each and every one of them.

* * *

Harrison woke with Jessica in his arms, her blonde hair flowing over his bare chest and the feeling of her warm soft breath on his skin as she slept soundly snuggled next to him. He didn't want that feeling to end. It was as if an angel had entered his life. An angel he'd never expected to meet.

Suddenly he noticed his cell phone light up. Concerned that it might be the hospital, he slipped from the warm bed and took his phone to the en suite bathroom. He didn't want to disturb Jessica if he needed to make an urgent call. He closed the door and opened the email icon and was instantly jolted into a reality he didn't expect or want.

Hi Harrison,

As you're a board member, I thought you should know that I just had a courtesy call from a colleague at the Eastern Memorial in Adelaide. Jessica was supposed to take on a locum role in six weeks' time, but it appears they are going to offer her the role of Acting Head of Paediatrics with a view to ongoing,

providing she's happy to start in one week's time. Sad to be losing her, but a huge opportunity for her in a hospital of that size. I guess we can't compete with that. We'll need to get a replacement as soon as possible.
All the best, Errol

Harrison froze. Jessica would be leaving much sooner than expected. Perhaps, if they'd been able to spend the full six weeks together, they might have been able to see where this was going, might have been able to lay down the foundations of something that had a future. But one week? Impossible. It was a done deal. She would not and should not decline the offer from a large teaching hospital. While Adelaide wasn't the other side of the world, he was a realist. With Jessica's new role, and with his workload and, more importantly, his son, the opportunity to progress their relationship to something more, something deeper didn't exist. And he didn't want to risk it. He wasn't about to make it more and then have it end. That would be dragging out the inevitable and he feared, with a woman like Jessica, he would only grow closer with every minute he spent with her.

Their connection was destined to be one night only and Harrison had no choice but to accept it.

He stepped into the shower, turned on the tap and let the hot water wash over him as he tried to erase the night before. He wanted more than anything to fall back into bed and make love to Jessica again, but he couldn't. She was perfect in almost every way. But one. She wasn't staying in town. And he didn't want to ask her to do it. He had no right to hold her back. He had to treat what they'd shared the night before as something casual. He couldn't let his heart lead his head again.

Jessica's early morning yawn morphed into a wide smile that she couldn't suppress. She stretched in the warmth of the king-sized bed, lifting her arms above her head, arching her back and pointing her toes. It was the most delicious feeling and she couldn't remember feeling that happy. Her mind drifted back to the tenderness and warmth in Harrison's kiss.

Her eyes wrinkled softly as her naked skin brushed against the sheets and she remembered the way he had brought every inch of her body to life.

She slid back under the covers, relishing the passion they had shared. Tingles spread over her body with the thought of his body bringing her such guilty pleasure. With a satisfied Cheshire cat grin, she thought back over the last week. So much had happened and, while not all of it appeared to be positive initially, the pendulum had swung back and with it brought so much more joy into her life than she'd thought possible. Harrison, she decided, was the type of man she could potentially fall hopelessly in love with and, surprisingly for her, she wasn't scared of those feelings. A few months ago she would have been so frightened she would have bolted from his bed, his home and, more than likely, the town if she had thought for a moment that she was developing feelings on any level for a man.

But Harrison had somehow changed that. Jessica wasn't sure how it had happened but he had made her feel safe enough to let down her guard and she wondered if, in the process, she might have found her knight in shining armour. She was definitely looking forward to a lot more nights with the country doctor.

And who knew what the future might bring? She thought back to the night before and what the Professor's wife had said about giving up the city life she knew for one in the country. Was that something Jessica could do? She wasn't sure but, the way she was feeling at that moment, she wasn't ruling it out either.

Jessica reminded herself there were still barriers to overcome. Did the country doctor need his heart mended just as much as she did or was his intact? Perhaps she didn't need to know it all. Not at first, at least, but she felt sure this time she wasn't falling for a man who would break her heart the way it had been broken before.

It had been the most amazing night. Ever. Harrison was the most wonderful lover. Giving and tender, yet demanding and strong. He was as complex in bed as he was out of it and that excited her. The night had been so special, so wonderful and she didn't want to allow anything to spoil it. Not the sadness of her past or question marks hanging over the future. She wanted to enjoy whatever it was they had right now and not block out what also might be.

Harrison had slipped from the bed before Jessica had woken. She could hear the shower running and suddenly felt a little disappointed that he hadn't remained in bed. Waking in his arms and making love again would have made the morning as perfect as the night had been, but she knew he was rostered on at the hospital so it was understandable. She hoped she would wake up the next morning in his bed and that he would stay in it with her for many hours.

Quickly but reluctantly, Jessica climbed from the warm, delightfully crumpled bed and gathered her underwear, hosiery and her dress, strewn over the highly polished floors. One by one she picked up the pieces. She would shower at home as she liked the scent of his skin on hers and wasn't in a hurry to wash him away.

'I'm sorry I had to get up but I need to get to work…and I have a stop to make before that.'

Jessica turned to find Harrison standing in the doorway, a plush grey towel hanging low on his hips. Dangerously low. In the soft hue of the morning light his chiselled chest made him look larger than life. Like a Greek statue. Carved and bronze and perfect. It took all of her self-control not to remove her clothes and suggest he call in sick so they could remain under the covers for another few hours.

'I understand completely,' she told him as she averted her eyes and, showing a great deal of restraint, stepped into her dress, the last piece of her clothing that had been thrown across the room the night before. She wasn't sure what he'd meant by *a stop to make before that*. Perhaps he had a patient home visit.

All things considered, she thought as she looked down at her outfit from the night before, she wasn't as dishevelled as she could and should have been. With any luck, her walk of shame might not be noticed by the neighbours after all.

'I wish I could ask you to stay but I have to...'

'Work, I know,' she said, cutting in nervously. Suddenly what they had shared seemed a lifetime ago. In a perfect world he would scoop her up and lay her on the bed and kiss her and tell her that he was falling madly in love with her. But they didn't live in a perfect world. 'It's all good. I have a million things to do today so I need to leave anyway.'

'Last night was great.'

'Yes, it was,' Jessica agreed, suddenly feeling uneasy about the tone of his voice. In the light of day, she sensed that Harrison wanted to put some distance between them. Both emotionally and physically. Perhaps the early morning shower was his way of breaking their intimacy. Waking in each other's arms would have put a very different slant on the situation. He looked ill-at-ease and she sensed it had nothing to do with his nakedness.

His behaviour confused her. He'd been so very certain about everything the night before. He'd been in command and now he looked unsure. She felt a little sick in the stomach by his sudden need to detach.

'I think you're amazing, Jessica,' he began,

breaking the strained moment of silence but not bridging the gap she now felt between them.

Jessica felt her heart sink. Only moments before, she had believed she was teetering on something close to falling in love with him but she feared that was not how he saw the situation. She had wanted him so badly that it frightened her and she had let down her guard, only to have him almost disregard it.

'Would you like breakfast or coffee?' he asked as he crossed to his wardrobe. 'I can make you some scrambled eggs once I'm dressed.'

Jessica drew a breath, trying to calm her emotions. She felt a stab of painful aware-ness. Was she the only one thinking past one night together?

'I think I might leave now,' she said hastily as she felt a tightness in her chest.

'Okay,' he agreed as he laid his clothes on the bed and began dressing. Within moments he donned dark blue jeans, a warm checked shirt and bulky camel sweater.

Jessica had never seen a man dress so

quickly. Not that she had seen a man get dressed after a one-night stand as it wasn't something she had done before, but the process did seem hurried. And extremely awkward, considering only hours before that she'd been naked in his bed.

'I'll see you at the hospital on Monday then?' she asked, hoping that he would ask to see her that night. If he did then she would know that she was reading the situation incorrectly. She wanted with all her heart to be proved wrong. So she gave him the opportunity to invite her over again.

'Yes, of course,' he replied. 'I'll see you Monday.'

She was mortified. Her reading was correct.

She'd hoped he might try to convince her to stay but he didn't. He was letting her walk away. She suddenly felt very empty. Even more empty than before she'd slept with him. Before she'd met him. And, unfortunately, those feelings told her that she had given at least a small piece of her heart to him. She'd hoped he deserved it but she was beginning to think perhaps he didn't. She wished it didn't cause an ache inside her, to be walking away from the night they'd shared with no promise of another.

The pain was growing by the minute and heightened as he walked her to the front door. The very place he had first kissed her the night before. The passion in his first kiss, the way he'd carried her into his bedroom and the love they made… It was all gone. He was letting her walk away as if it meant nothing.

What they'd shared was just a one-night stand after all. She hadn't thought that was all it would be as she had lain in his arms but perhaps that was just what he did—made a woman feel there was more without saying it—and perhaps it was unintentional. She was confused and felt let down. She knew she had no right to expect more, Harrison had not promised more, but it still felt wrong to be almost asked to leave.

Was she missing something? Was there something about Harrison she didn't know? She wasn't sure but she was teetering on something close to heartbreak and she didn't need another heartbreak. It didn't take long for Jessica to realise that spending the night with him was quite possibly the biggest mistake she had made in a very long time.

Harrison turned to her as he unlocked the front door. His eyes were filled with emotion that Jessica couldn't define.

'I'll always think of last night as special.'

Jessica couldn't find any words to say. She was just trying to hold back tears that were welling deep inside and threatening to spill onto her cheeks.

'I know you're not planning on staying in town and, believe me, I wouldn't expect or ask you to change your plans, based on one night together. I just want you to know that I think you're an amazing woman, Jessica. Any man would be fortunate to have you in his life. I'm truly sorry the way our lives are destined to be, and that it can't be me.'

CHAPTER EIGHT

JESSICA DROVE HOME in shock. Afterwards, she couldn't remember leaving Harrison's house or driving the short distance to her own rental home. She shouldn't have been on the road, she realised, when she arrived at her door. Her mind was a fog and she had driven in a complete daze. There had been no one on the road and perhaps that was why the drive was so forgettable or perhaps it was because she was so preoccupied with thoughts of the man who had just ended something between them before it had a chance.

She was angry, and sad, and confused and blindsided and…a dozen different emotions she didn't know she could feel. All of them caused by Harrison Wainwright. Why the hell had he invited her home? Was it just to spend one night together? Had he planned all along to kiss her goodbye in the morning for no good reason? Walk her to the door and not want to see her again?

And then to give her a line if translated into Italian would be worthy of a place in an opera. Or at the very least a soap opera. *Any man would be fortunate to have you in his life... I'm truly sorry...it can't be me.* Who said that? And why? And what did he mean by *the way our lives are destined to be*?

His parting words were coming back to her in a jumbled mess. Her mind was racing at a million miles an hour as she threw her overcoat on the sofa and unzipped her dress and stepped out of it and tossed it on top of her discarded coat before she made her way to the bathroom.

The house was as cold as ice but her blood was boiling as she thought back over their conversations. She wanted to wash any trace of the man from her skin—the scent of his cologne, the scent of his body, she wanted none of it. She turned on the shower and stepped into the steaming water and scrubbed her body with a loofah. All the while she pushed visions of Harrison from her mind and tried to erase the feeling of his arms around her. She couldn't trust that, but the ache in her heart was more real than she cared to admit.

What had gone wrong? Was he really just another bad man? And was she a magnet for men who thought nothing further than how she could meet their own desires?

Or was it her? Was it the barriers she had up when they'd first met? Surely when she was lying in Harrison's bed he would have known the barriers were down. All of them. She reached for the shampoo and, putting her head under the running water, began to wash her hair. His cologne was in her hair and she wanted nothing to remind her of him, nothing to unexpectedly take her back to the hours they'd spent together. Her life felt as if it was unravelling again. The very reason why she'd promised herself not to get involved. She had sworn off men for a very good reason.

Suddenly she thought back to when she'd mentioned she wasn't the marrying kind to Harrison that first day at the hospital. Perhaps she'd made him think she was the one-night stand type with the whole, *I'm not a picket fence kind of woman* statement? But then, the way Rachel Naughton spoke about him, as the doting godfather of her daughter, he was a man who needed a good woman to share his life with. That was not close to a description of the man who'd as good as told her to leave his house the morning after seducing her.

Jessica was close to going mad. She had woken a happy woman, luxuriating in the feeling of what she and Harrison had shared the night before, and now, in the light of day, she was berating herself for going home with him. Maybe she should have taken it more slowly. Maybe she should have said no. Maybe they'd rushed into something that just as quickly had turned into nothing.

As she turned off the shower she told herself that the *maybes* had to stop—she was grasping at straws.

She had to accept they had shared a night. That was where it had started and that was where it would end.

She just had to find a way to erase it from her mind.

* * *

Her weekend was filled with thoughts that bounced from regret to acceptance and then back again. It involved a lot of ice cream and more than one call to Cassey, who consoled her and thankfully did not mention online dating as a solution. They made plans to catch up when Jessica was back in Sydney or Cassey made it over to Adelaide.

It was about ten o'clock on Sunday night when she received an email that she wasn't expecting, but one that inadvertently changed the course of her life, even before she received it. It was regarding the role at the Eastern Memorial Hospital in Adelaide. Not as the locum Paediatric Consultant as she had planned in a few weeks but, due to an unexpected resignation, offering the position of Acting Head of Paediatrics if Jessica was interested. There was an opportunity to trial the role for three months and then, if she was successful, the potential to be transitioned into the ongoing position. But the conditions were non-negotiable. She needed to be in Adelaide by Monday of the following week. There was no shifting the time line if she was to accept the position.

It was a role she had dreamed of for so many years and an offer she hadn't expected in her wildest dreams. While she should have been excited by the prospect of achieving a lifelong goal and the opportunities it brought, instead she read and reread the email and thought of it purely as an escape route. There was no elation. Her emotions were flatlined.

Ordinarily she would ask for more time so she could complete her current contract or at least give two weeks' notice, but now those terms more than suited her. Leaving a position with little warning was not what she liked to do and she hoped that Professor Langridge and the hospital Board would understand. What the Head of ER thought didn't matter in the slightest to her. He had not reached out for two days. There had been nothing from him. It was as if nothing had happened between them.

As much as she wanted to accept the new position immediately, Jessica decided to give Errol the courtesy of advising him of her plans in person the next day.

* * *

It was two in the afternoon before she could get in to see the Professor.

'I'm not going to lie; I'm very sad to see you go. We've been trying to secure funding to keep you on here, as everyone working with you is so thrilled to have had you on board and they've told me in person. You've made quite an impression with everyone in the space of a week. Particularly with Harrison Wainwright. He's got to be your biggest fan and the keenest that you should be kept on board.'

Jessica shot the Professor a rueful look but said nothing. The irony of it all. The man who was her supposed biggest advocate was the one who'd hastened her decision to leave.

'In saying that, Harrison was quite adamant that we didn't force your hand or coerce you in any way. From day one, he wanted it to be your choice or not at all.'

Jessica was not buying into anything said by or about Harrison Wainwright. None of it held water in her mind any more and she put it out to the universe that if it could arrange for her to avoid seeing him or hearing his voice for the rest of the week, she would be very grateful.

'Well, again, I'm also sad in many ways but I have to think about my career at this stage in my life and the opportunity to be Head of Paediatrics in Adelaide is just too good to refuse.' *And a damn good exit strategy from Harrison*, she thought.

'It is an amazing opportunity,' came a voice from the doorway. A voice that Jessica recognised only too well. It was the voice of someone who had only a few nights before shared pillow talk with her. 'Too good to refuse, I agree.'

Jessica felt her heart sink, hearing his voice again.

'With your skills and mindset, Jessica, you were never destined to stay long in this town.' With that Harrison exited as quickly as he had appeared.

'A man of few words, our Harrison.'

Jessica didn't respond. In her opinion, Harrison could certainly say all the right words when it suited him.

'We have you on board until Friday then?' Errol asked with a hopeful lilt to his voice.

'I could make it six and work through until late Saturday if that would help? I can arrange flights and accommodation in Adelaide and fly to Sydney and then directly on to Adelaide on Sunday. I'm not starting there until Monday.'

'That's very good of you but certainly cutting it close.'

'Not at all. I'm truly sorry to be leaving early but, all things considered, it's for the best.'

Jessica left Errol's office feeling torn. Letting down the Board and Errol had never been in her plans but then neither was falling for the Head of ER and having her heart broken. All things taken into account, she was doing as well as she could to remain on for another six days. She hoped that Harrison would give her the space to do her job and leave with her dignity intact. She didn't want to tell him what she thought of him or ask for an explanation beyond the empty excuse he'd provided before she'd left his home because that would be letting him know how much he had come to mean to her in a very short space of time. And how she'd mistakenly thought she had come to mean something to him too.

The week passed by quickly. She sent her signed acceptance letter to Eastern Memorial and then organised her flights for the following Sunday morning. It was a nine o'clock flight from Armidale to Sydney with a two-hour layover and an eleven o'clock flight from Sydney to Adelaide. It wasn't difficult to secure an apartment close to the hospital, which meant she wouldn't need to organise a car as she could use public transport and cabs and look into purchasing a car later if needed.

Being organised felt good. Being in control of her destiny felt even better. While the idea of staying in one place was a little daunting after a year of moving around, there was the three-month trial period in the terms of the contract and that was reassuring to her. She might like being in one place, as long as that place was not near Harrison. And if she didn't like being settled, then she would decline the

ongoing role and return to her nomadic exis-
tence.

It was her second to last day and she had
visited all the staff to thank them, as many
would not be on duty over the weekend. They
had wanted to host a farewell afternoon tea
but Jessica declined. While the sentiment was
lovely, having to see Harrison at the event and
receive his best wishes, or knowing that he
might have chosen not to attend, would be far
too awkward. And more than a little sad. She
found a lovely scarf and beautiful card signed
by many of the staff in her office on the Friday
night, which she considered was too much for
having only been there such a short time. She
intended on sending a thank you note from
Adelaide. Harrison's name was on the card
but his message was brief and nothing could
be read into it by anyone, including Jessica.

Walking to her car that night, Jessica felt
so many mixed emotions, but predominantly
sadness and a sense of loss. She had one more
day before she turned her back on the town
she knew she would never visit again.

'Jessica, wait.'

She turned to find Harrison standing only a few feet from her.

'I don't want it to end like this,' he told her.

Jessica stared at the man who had broken her heart—and before she'd met him she hadn't even known her heart had mended enough to love again.

'How did you want it to end?'

'Not at all, to be honest, but I knew it had to.'

Jessica shook her head. She wasn't buying anything he was saying but she was confused why he had bothered to chase her down.

'You are bigger than this town. You deserve this opportunity in Adelaide.'

'Please don't tell me that you know what I deserve after what happened.'

'I did what I thought was best…'

'For yourself. One night with me and you were done. I stupidly thought that what we shared meant something…' she began and then stopped.

'It did but there was no point trying to make it something more. You were always going to leave.'

'I don't want to talk about it any more,' she said, holding back tears.

'No matter what you think now, I want you to understand before you go that the night we shared did mean something.'

'Sure,' she said as she turned and walked away. *But not enough to ask me to stay.*

It was just after ten the following evening. Jessica's last day in Armidale and she was watching television and thinking about heading to bed. The day had gone well. She had not seen Harrison and that brought both sadness and relief to her.

She had closed the chapter on what they had shared.

She looked over at her suitcase and carry-on bag; both were packed and she felt a sense of organisation coming back to her life. A nice pair of trousers, a shirt and jacket for the plane trip were hanging in her room for the trip. If the cases were lost again, she wouldn't be turning up in jeans and a jumper on her first day in Adelaide. She had learnt that lesson the hard way in Armidale. Along with another one. She would lock her heart away for ever.

Suddenly her phone vibrated on the table. She picked it up and saw it was the hospital. She wondered if she had left something there.

'Dr Ayers, it's Jane from ER.'

'Hello, Jane, is everything all right?'

'No, not really. We have a young boy who has presented at the hospital with suspected appendicitis. I'm sorry to bother you; I know you're no longer on staff and you're leaving Armidale tomorrow morning but this is an emergency.'

'Isn't Dr Wainwright on tonight in ER?'

'Yes.'

'Then I'm a little confused as to why you need me. I'm sure Dr Wainwright can handle the case. Unless he has a particularly heavy patient load this evening.'

'No, we've only got two other patients but he's asked me to call you, especially. He knows it's late but he's hoping you might be able to come in and assess the young boy. He said he can meet you in the car park so you don't walk in the dark alone.'

'Please tell him that I don't need him to meet me anywhere. But what I do need is to understand why I'm required. Are there complications? I need some context to this request.'

'I'll pass you on to Dr Wainwright…'

'No, don't do that,' Jessica cut in but it was too late. The last thing she wanted was to hear his voice before she went to bed. She didn't want to be kept awake by thoughts of him. She was doing her best to forget she'd ever laid eyes on him.

The nurse had handed the phone over. 'Jessica, it's Harrison.'

Jessica took a deep breath to steady her nerves. She hadn't thought she'd ever hear his voice again.

'Jessica, are you there?' he asked.

'Yes, Harrison; what's this about? It's late and I don't understand why I'm needed. You have enough experience with suspected appendicitis.'

'I have, Jessica, but this case is quite different. Believe me, I wouldn't be disturbing you if it wasn't urgent.'

'Why—what's different about this patient?

Why can't you manage him with the resources you have?'

'Because…' Harrison began and paused '…because, Jessica, he's my son.'

Jessica was dumbfounded and almost dropped her phone. Harrison had a son? They had spoken at length and he'd never thought to mention he had a son? That was a significant piece of information to have kept to himself. Why had he hidden that from her? She felt sick to the stomach. How could she have got it all so wrong? She'd thought she knew him but she didn't know him at all. Why would he hide something so significant from her? He had chosen what he wanted to tell her and clearly kept a number of things to himself. Suddenly he was a father. Where was the child when she'd stayed over? God, how could she have been so stupid to fall for someone like him? Again, she had chosen a man who had lied to her by avoiding a hugely important detail about his life.

'Jessica?' Harrison's voice on the line brought her back to his call. He needed something or, more accurately, his son did.

'Where was your son the other night?'

'At my parents'. They look after him when I…'

'Have women sleep over. So, what happened between us was premeditated on your part?' Jessica told him flatly.

'No, I didn't plan any of what happened between us…nor do I regret it.'

'Then that makes one of us, because I do,' she spat back angrily. 'And, while we're being honest, do you have a wife as well?'

Harrison did not reply to her question. There was nothing but a deafening silence on the line.

'Oh, my God, you do. You have a wife and a son!' She'd thought she couldn't feel worse than the morning she had left his home but she realised she could, because she suddenly did.

'Bryce's mother is overseas.'

'So that makes it okay to sleep with me? An ocean apart means what happened between us doesn't count?' Jessica felt her blood run cold. Harrison had a wife and he had the audacity to admit it now. It was Jessica's worst nightmare all over again. She felt herself spinning close to the edge and could barely breathe. 'I slept with a married man.' *Again.*

'Stop, please, Jessica; it's not like that. You didn't sleep with a married man. Bryce's mother lives overseas. We're only days away from the divorce being finalised.'

'I don't believe you.'

'It's true. I wouldn't lie to you.'

'Really? You never told me you had a son before now. You led me to believe you were single.'

'I'm a single father, Jessica. Well... I will be by next week. You didn't sleep with a married man. You slept with a single father.'

'This is all getting too complicated,' she told him with her mind struggling to process everything she had heard. 'Even if it's true, why didn't you mention your son to me? There were plenty of opportunities.'

'I guess I was just protecting him.'

'You were protecting your son from a paediatrician?'

'I know that sounds ridiculous...'

'Because it is.'

Harrison hesitated again. 'I had my reasons, maybe stupid ones, but…'

'Don't go there,' she said angrily. 'Let it go. I'm past it, Harrison.'

'I will go there later. I'm not letting you think that any of what I did or said or didn't say was about you. It was me and I'm trying to let go of the past, I really am.'

Jessica was still not convinced. 'Please just tell me what you want.'

Harrison drew a breath. 'My son is in the ER now. I need a second opinion from a doctor of your calibre. Believe me, I didn't want to put this pressure on you but you're the best doctor I know. I'm worried.'

'There's really no point us talking about this…'

'Please, Jessica.'

'I mean there's no point us talking because I'm on my way…but, just so you know, I'm doing this for your son, not you.' With that, Jessica hung up and grabbed her car keys and overcoat. Despite how she felt about Harrison, she would be there for his son.

* * *

Harrison was waiting in the dark car park for her but she chose to ignore any recognition of chivalry, asking only for the cold hard facts about his son's condition. There was nothing more between them.

'Thank you for coming out.'

'Again, this is because I love children and it's why I chose paediatrics. This has nothing to do with how I feel about you. If it did, I'm not so sure I would be here.' Jessica walked briskly in the direction of the main doors of the hospital.

'I know I deserve your reaction,' he told her. 'And, as soon as I can, I want to explain why I behaved the way I did. I owe you that.'

Jessica drew a strained breath, not from the pace of their walking, instead from having to be around Harrison. She'd thought she would never have to lay eyes upon him again and that had suited her just fine. She struggled to speak now, as being near him had brought back so much of what she wanted to forget, but she knew she needed to channel her lingering anger to get through whatever lay ahead. She didn't want to hear his excuses because there was nothing to be gained from it.

'I'm past that, Harrison. I don't care about your reasons. It means nothing to me now. What I care about, in fact *all* I care about, is your son. Nothing else.'

'I'm truly grateful...'

'Please, I don't want to hear anything close to that from you. Just give me the background now,' she said as she picked up speed to get inside. It was starting to rain and she didn't want another of Harrison's chivalrous yet shallow gestures of perhaps taking off his jacket to shield her. She would rather drown.

'Bryce was complaining of a pain in his stomach last weekend and then he lost his appetite. I incorrectly assumed it was nerves about starting school and me being overseas recently.'

'What else?' she asked, filtering out all the superfluous information. Adrenalin was kicking in. There was a little boy's life potentially at stake.

'The pain subsided during the week, so I thought nothing more of it, but it started again yesterday morning and escalated during the day.'

'Understandable, stomach aches are not un-usual at that age, but you wouldn't have called me here at this hour if it wasn't serious, so tell me all of the symptoms and the time frame. Any diarrhoea?'

'My mother picked him up when the school called her around lunchtime. He'd soiled his pants and was very embarrassed. The school nurse cleaned him and provided him with some second-hand clothing but, understand-ably, he wanted to go home,' he replied as they entered the automatic doors of the hospital and continued at breakneck speed into ER. 'He's been at their house for two nights, as he al-ways is if I'm on a late shift, and they didn't want to bother me. They thought it was some-thing he ate. My father finally called me two hours ago when he saw Bryce struggling to get out of the bath and walk into his bedroom. My father's retired but was a military doctor and knew something wasn't right.'

Jessica looked him up and down and didn't hide her disdain. He had an entire family in the town and he'd never bothered to say a thing. She wasn't his keeper and they hadn't known each other for long but, in Jessica's mind, in an open and honest conversation some, if not all, these things would have come up unless he was purposely hiding them.

'Jessica, I know I've screwed up everything with us and I will try to explain and, if I can, make it up to you but right now I need your help.'

'And you have it. I'm here to help.' At odds with how she was feeling, her voice was unemotional. 'He's five years of age, is that correct?'

'Yes, five years and three months.' He intuitively followed suit, kept to the facts and dropped any reference to them.

'Any other medical conditions?' she asked as they entered the ER.

'No. He's your average young boy. Good weight for his height. The pain has escalated so he's on IV pain relief.'

Jessica quickly scrubbed in, donned a gown

and gloves and entered the bay to find a little version of Harrison lying on the bed in a tiny hospital gown. The similarity was uncanny and a little unnerving.

Calmly she approached the little boy. 'Hello, Bryce. I'm Dr Jessica. I work at the hospital with your daddy and I heard you had a tummy ache.'

'Uh-huh, it was bad but the medicine made it better.'

'Was it very bad?' she asked, noting the IV that was administering pain relief.

'Very, very bad,' Bryce replied with the saddest of faces.

'May I have a look at you and try to find out why your tummy's hurting?'

Bryce nodded his mop of thick black hair, again just like his father's.

Pushing away the clear similarities, Jessica continued, 'Did you feel pain anywhere else?'

'Just my tummy, near my belly button.'

Jessica turned to the nurse. 'Is there any fever?'

'His temperature is slightly elevated. Thirty-nine point five.'

'More than likely from the infection,' Jessica replied as she took a stethoscope, warmed it in the palm of her hand for a moment then listened to his chest. Happy with what she could hear, she turned to the nurse again. 'Have you taken bloods to see if the white cell count is elevated?'

'Yes, just waiting on the lab now.'

'We may not have time to wait for that result; please go and put a rush on them.'

The nurse raced from the bay, leaving Harrison and Jessica alone with Bryce.

'Can he raise his right leg?'

'Not without pain,' Harrison replied. 'That was the catalyst for me calling you.'

Gently she lifted Bryce down and began an external examination. There was extra tenderness on his lower right side and nothing elsewhere in his abdomen. She gently replaced the gown and, once the nurse returned, Jessica signalled to Harrison to step outside the bay with her.

'Bryce is presenting with many of the symptoms of appendicitis—the raised temperature, diarrhoea and tenderness near the site. It's not overly common in someone of Bryce's age, but also not unheard of. I think we need to consider an emergency appendectomy rather than risking it rupturing overnight,' she told him as she pulled her gloves free.

'It can't wait till the morning?' Harrison questioned her.

'From what you're telling me, the symptoms have been present for a few days, if not a week already, so my educated guess is we don't have that much time to decide. The bacteria are rapidly multiplying and, with that pressure, Bryce's appendix could rupture.'

'There's still the possibility that it's not appendicitis.'

'There's always a possibility with any diagnosis but for me that possibility is too small,' she countered. She could sense the fear in Harrison's voice and understood why he had those doubts but she had to push back. Erring on the side of caution was riskier than operating. 'Fairly soon, if I'm right, the decision will be made for us and if that happens then we'll have a whole different set of issues, including the risk to other organs from the resulting peritonitis. And then the emergency surgery will be far more complicated.'

'What would you do in my place?'

'I just told you...'

'Jessica—' he cut in, then continued in a very controlled manner '—I want to know what you'd do if you were not his doctor, but instead his mother. What decision would you make then? Jessica, I'm scared, more scared than I've ever been. I don't want to get this wrong. I can't lose my boy. I need your help.'

Jessica was knocked sideways by Harrison's honesty and vulnerability. Only a few hours before she hadn't known Harrison had a son, and now he was asking her what decision would she make if she was the boy's mother. She wasn't anyone's mother and might never be, so the question was a difficult one. Even more so coming from Harrison. But, as a paediatrician, it wasn't the first time she had been asked a question like this. And each time she understood it wasn't to absolve the parent of their responsibility; it was just a question about gaining perspective. This time was very different though because it was being asked by a man who a few days ago she'd thought might be her world, her future, her everything. A man who'd made her believe in her own judgement and love again, for the briefest of times. But he was also a man who'd turned his back on her. A man who'd broken her heart. And one she wanted to hate. But now, standing so near and learning more, she found that hard to do.

'Harrison, I know it's overwhelming to make a decision for someone you love, but you're the only one who can make it. And if he was my son—' she paused and drew a breath '—I would make the decision to operate tonight.'

Harrison nodded. She could see there was still a battle raging in his head and his heart as he clenched his fingers and an anxious tic stirred in his jaw.

'Then that's what we'll do,' he told her.

'You've made the right decision,' she said and, instinctively and without thinking, she placed her bare hand on his arm in a comforting and reassuring way.

'I hope so,' he said, suddenly putting his hand over hers.

Jessica froze. She hadn't expected that reaction. From a parent, she would understand and not react, but the feeling of Harrison's warm skin against hers brought memories flooding back—memories that she didn't want to deal with again. She pulled her hand free; she was the one who needed space now.

'Do we have a surgeon on call?' she asked back in the direction of the bay where Bryce was waiting.

'Normally we have two general surgeons on call but unfortunately Dr Franklin is down with influenza and Dr Douglas is in Tamworth overnight. He's due back in the morning. It wouldn't usually be a problem because, normally, I would be able to cover.'

'Okay. That certainly changes things.'

'Would you prefer us to hold off and monitor overnight?' Harrison asked as he began pacing.

'No. I understand you want conservative treatment, that's always my aim with my patients, but in this case moderate might, as I said before, be the far riskier option at this point. In the absence of any other choice, it looks like you and I are operating on your son. It's unorthodox at best but it's Bryce's best chance. Have you undertaken an appendectomy recently?'

'One, a few months ago, in similar circumstances.'

'And the age of the patient?'

'Twenty-nine.'

'Twenty-nine, and Bryce is five, so this procedure will be the same...but also very different. You know what I mean. So I'll take the lead. Are you good with that?' Her look was serious as she was preparing mentally for the task at hand. Saving Harrison's son, with his assistance.

'Of course.'

'Bryce,' Harrison said softly as they both re-entered the ER bay. 'Your stomach ache is not going to get any better unless Dr Jessica operates and takes out your appendix.'

'What's that?'

'A little piece of your tummy that you don't need but it is sick and has germs stuck in it and it's giving you the stomach ache.'

'Will the operation hurt?'

'No, you will be asleep and afterwards the nurses will give you medicine to make it better.'

'Then they should give medicine so I don't need an operation, Daddy.'

Harrison appreciated his son's logic. It wasn't correct but it would seem sensible to a five-year-old.

'I wish we could but your appendix is hurting you because it is sick and it needs to be taken out of your tummy. It won't get well with medicine.'

'Will it be put in a jar like Toby's tonsils? He brought the jar in for show and tell.'

'Maybe. We can talk about it later, but first things first and that is getting the sick appendix out of you. And I'll be right with you the whole time.'

'You promise you won't leave me?'

Harrison dropped down to eye level with his son. 'I promise you I'll be right by you. I'm not going anywhere.'

The theatre was prepared and the anaesthesiologist, Dr Martin Barry, arrived fifteen minutes later and was given an overview by Jessica of how she saw the surgery proceeding. She told him that she hoped it would be straightforward laparoscopic procedure and, if so, should be completed within thirty minutes. If there were complications it could take a little longer and they would be prepared for that too.

While Bryce was prepped for surgery, Harrison and Jessica headed in to scrub for the single most important surgical procedure that Harrison would perform in his life. With the water running, they both lathered up and then with the assistance of theatre staff, slipped on gloves, gown, cap and glasses.

'If it becomes too much being in there with your son,' Jessica began, 'please just leave the theatre. Don't hesitate. I can do it alone but it will be better if you at least begin the procedure with me as I'm not entirely sure what we will find going in. It's exploratory and, with any luck, we will find an ever so slightly infected organ that we can take out quickly without any drama and then Bryce will be running around again by next weekend.'

'Let's hope so.'

'At this stage, hoping is all we can do.'

They entered the theatre, where Bryce was resting under the effects of some pre-operative medication with the rest of the late-night surgical team busily preparing for the impending surgical procedure around him. Dr Barry had adjusted the dose of anaesthesia for his height and weight and age as noted on his patient records.

'Daddy's here, just as I promised, with Dr Jessica,' Harrison told the sleepy boy. 'And I'll still be here when you wake up.'

Slowly the little boy drifted into an unconscious state from the anaesthesia.

'You are good to go,' Dr Barry told her.

'Okay, let's get this appendix out and make this young man feel like himself again,' she said as she took the laparoscopic intra-abdominal trocar from the nurse and began the keyhole surgery by making an incision for the umbilical port. Once the trocar had been inserted into the umbilical port, gas was then gently pumped into Bryce's abdomen to inflate the area to enable Jessica to see more clearly what they were facing. Harrison inserted the laparoscope and Jessica could see immediately that the appendix was red and inflamed.

'You were right about the appendix...' Harrison began and then stopped.

Jessica was correct about the appendicitis but there was more and it wasn't good. The theatre staff could all see on the monitor that Bryce's appendix had perforated and the infected contents had spilled out, covering the other organs in his abdomen.

Jessica was concerned but she wasn't going to let Harrison know and she quickly pulled herself back to the task at hand.

'Will we need to change to open surgery?' the theatre nurse asked, preparing to wheel over the other surgical trolley.

'No, I'll continue as planned. I'll insert the other two trocars, then utilise them as a passage into the cavity for the other instruments. I will dissect out the ruptured appendix and mobilise it.'

Jessica gently moved the appendix to one

side using the grasper so that she could investigate further his tiny abdomen.

'I can see where it's ruptured; the tissue is necrotic and turning black from the infection,' she explained.

'That is not an overnight occurrence,' Harrison said flatly. 'This is a slightly longer-term infection.'

'Children are good at covering up sometimes, Harrison,' she told him, sensing he was feeling a level of guilt for his son's condition. 'I'll staple off just below the rupture. It will divide the appendix and leave a row of staples across the stump.' Jessica fired one row of staples to divide the appendix from the colon. 'The second row of staples will divide the blood supply,' she explained as she fired another row. 'The staples don't dissolve but they won't cause Bryce any pain or issues in the future.'

Using the graspers again, Jessica checked the staple lines across the stump seal were secure and that there was no leakage or bleeding from the colon. 'I will leave the appendix in there for a moment while I look into the pelvis.'

'There's a lot of pus and murky fluid,' Harrison said, visibly distraught but remaining calm. 'He must have been in so much pain.'

'A great deal, but he's clearly a strong boy,' Jessica responded. 'But after we clean all this fluid and pus out of his pelvis, he'll be feeling like a new little man.' Jessica inserted a suctioning tool and emptied the cavity of the infected material. 'Just to make sure there's nothing remaining there that we can't see, I'll put a drain down into the pelvis and bring it out through the skin. It will need to stay in for four days.'

Jessica ensured all was as she expected and there were no unexpected surprises. 'I can now take out the appendix through the incision.'

Once she had done so, the nurse took the draining tube and attached it to a bulb pump and then Jessica removed all three trocars and began to suture closed the three small wounds. Harrison watched on in awe of her skills. His gratitude was born of the fact that Jessica had saved his son's life; his respect was born of watching such a skilled surgeon.

'I'll leave the port valve in place too for a few days, along with the drain, so that gas can escape from his stomach. If we don't he'll have similar pain again but this time from the procedure.'

With that she stepped back and he watched as she walked from the theatre, leaving the nurses and anaesthesiologist to do their work and take Bryce to Recovery. Harrison chose to stay.

Her work was done.

And now she should be able to walk away… but suddenly her legs felt heavy and her stomach uneasy. Was she walking away from this town too soon? Was Harrison telling the truth? She wasn't sure about anything and she didn't know if she was making the right choice any more. She wondered if she needed to hear him out.

Seeing the depth of love that he had for his son, the trust and belief Harrison had placed in her, suddenly Jessica had more questions than she had answers.

He had based his decision about his son's surgery on what she had said she would do if she were Bryce's mother. An unexpected question and one that made her look at everything a little differently. Including him.

And how he saw her.

CHAPTER NINE

JESSICA FOUND HARRISON outside Bryce's room at six the next morning, understandably dishevelled from a night she suspected had been spent sitting up in a hospital chair. He was looking down at the ground, his head resting in his hands. Just as he'd promised, he'd not left his son's side. Jessica wasn't surprised. His love for his son was undeniable.

'Harrison,' she said softly, so as to not startle him, as she sat on the empty chair beside him. She had barely slept herself but at least what little sleep she'd managed was in her own bed. She was concerned about Bryce and confused about his father. And both had made her toss and turn and wonder if she should get on the plane and turn her back on the man who had hurt her.

Or whether she should stay and see if there was something there worth fighting for.

He raised his head and faced her. His gutted expression cut her to the core. She wished it didn't but it did. He was exposed and vulnerable and her heart went out to him. She wanted to find reasons to hate him. She wanted to not give a damn. But, sitting so close to him, she was struggling to find a reason to hate him—and she did give a damn.

But there was still so much she didn't understand.

'I had to step out. I needed a few minutes...'

'And some black coffee,' she added, handing him one she had picked up at the cafeteria. 'They told me you'd been here all night.'

'I couldn't go home. Bryce needed me here, and I needed to be here.'

'He'll pull through.' She knew they had made the right decision to operate and her earlier call to ICU had confirmed the prognosis for Bryce was optimistic.

The prognosis for her and Harrison was not so certain but she couldn't leave the way it was, with so many questions and so much left unsaid. There was unfinished business. If nothing else, Jessica knew she needed closure or what they had shared and what might have been would haunt her.

'He's all I have, Jessica. Every choice I've made about my life has been based on what's best for my son. I want to shield him from hurt for as long as I can. He's had enough in his life and he's not even fully aware of it yet. He'll have a lot of questions as he grows up and the answers might be painful for him to hear.'

Jessica listened intently, hoping that some of her questions might be answered. Was walking away from her, deciding one night was all they would be, one of those decisions? But why did he not want to see if there could be more? Why would he worry about his son being around her? She loved children and she had devoted her life to providing the best care for children.

'You put Bryce first; it's what devoted parents do,' she told him, wishing she could put her arms around him and comfort him but knowing she couldn't. She wasn't willing to risk showing that level of familiarity or intimacy. 'Bryce will be fine. He's a little fighter.'

'I've been fighting for custody of my son for the last five years.' He raked his hand through his hair. 'Going crazy thinking that I might lose him.'

Jessica was surprised to learn he had been battling to keep his son for so long. The child was only five years of age. She was beginning to understand his level of protectiveness over his son. Harrison had been a single dad for almost Bryce's entire life.

'And now, when I finally get custody, I almost lose him. He was in so much pain and I hesitated. I wanted to leave it until morning. What sort of father does that?'

'One who cares and thinks about things thoroughly and weighs up the risks,' she countered. 'One who doesn't rush in.'

'Oh, I've rushed into things before.'

'Maybe you've learnt a hard lesson about it and that's why you didn't want to rush this time?'

Harrison looked up at the ceiling and drew a deep and thoughtful breath. 'Maybe. But sometimes you have to make quick decisions and hope on a wing and a prayer you get it right.'

'Sometimes you do.' She agreed. *Like the one she had made that morning in coming to see Harrison.*

'If it wasn't for you encouraging me not to be conservative, peritonitis would have most definitely set in overnight and then...' He paused. 'I don't want to think what might have happened. I just wish that I'd acted sooner...'

'There's no point wishing,' Jessica cut in. 'I learnt that a long time ago. You have to accept the situation you're facing and make the right decision at the time with what you know. And afterwards there's no point in looking back because you can't do anything about it. That's what we did last night when we operated.'

'But if only I'd taken more notice of the symptoms two days ago...'

'Harrison, you have to stop this. Look at me. Remember, you can't look back. Bryce is a tough little boy, he managed to hide a simmering appendix from you, and there's no point with the *if only*. God knows, I've spent the best part of a year questioning myself over the mistakes I've made and it doesn't undo what's done.'

Harrison lifted his head and looked at Jessica. His eyes were heavy and tired and filled with fear and something else she couldn't define. 'Jessica, you should have no regrets about anything. I'm the one that should have regrets…particularly where you and I are concerned. Any man would be so lucky to have you and I messed up. I wasn't thinking straight,' he said, his hand moving closer to hers.

Instinctively, Jessica moved her hand out of his reach. It wasn't something she did out of anger. More the need to keep some boundaries for a little longer.

'But I thought I had to push you away, for your sake and mine,' he said, drawing a deep and thoughtful breath.

'I'm not sure I understand. I mean I know you've been in a battle for Bryce, but that has nothing to do with me.'

'I know, absolutely nothing to do with you. It's just that I worried there wasn't enough in this town to hold your interest and I don't want to start something, only to have it end because it wasn't the right thing for you.'

'I love this town, it's amazing and the hospital is as advanced as any I've worked in. Why would you say that?'

'I'm done with convincing anyone that this is where they want to be. I did it once and it ended badly.' He was wringing his hands and staring into another time and place.

Jessica hesitated, then decided there was nothing to lose in knowing the truth. 'Are you talking about Bryce's mother?'

'Yes. I don't think I can face doing it again. Convince you to stay and see where this might lead when you really want to be somewhere, anywhere other than this town. And if it isn't what you want, when you walk away after a few months you won't just take a piece of my heart, you'd take a big piece of Bryce's heart with you. It's not fair for him to pay the price again for his father falling in love too quickly.'

Falling in love? Jessica fell back against the hard chair of the waiting area. He had just said he was falling in love with her? Were his feelings as strong for her as her feelings had been for him? She looked at him, saying nothing, just wanting to know more about what drove him and what made him the man he was.

'I met Bryce's mother and we rushed into a relationship. She was a make-up artist in town for six weeks for a film shoot and we met, hit it off and thought it was love at first sight. One thing led to another and she found out she was pregnant.' He stopped and took a deep purposeful breath. 'It shouldn't have happened, we took precautions, but nothing is one hundred per cent effective. I have Bryce and I wouldn't change anything but his mother didn't feel the same way. I convinced her to stay in Armidale, marry me and raise our son.'

'That was very chivalrous and a little old-fashioned of you.'

'It was the right thing to do and I thought we could be happy and for a while I thought we were. We had our differences but, for the main part, I thought everything was okay until Bryce was three months old and she announced that she was *bored beyond belief with country life*…and me. Those were her words, and they stayed with me. She hated everything about her life here and said she would go mad if she had to stay even another week. That was it; she was leaving.'

'That's such a cruel thing to say to anyone.'

'It was how she felt; she didn't hold back.'

'Did she try and take Bryce?'

'No. She didn't want him. Strangely, while I'm glad she didn't fight me for him initially, it hurt even more that she didn't want Bryce. I couldn't understand it. But over the years she sporadically threatened to take him. If I asked her to make the effort to visit and keep a level of maternal contact that would be beneficial to Bryce as he grew up, she would tell me she was taking him to live with her. It wasn't ever going to be her raising him; it was going to be her parents, who live in San Diego. So I eased off asking her to factor her son into her life.'

Jessica shook her head. 'I don't know what to say. I don't understand how she could not want her baby and then use him to manipulate the situation.'

'She believed that having a child would hold her back. She kept reminding me that she was a city girl, born and bred in Los Angeles, and this town could never compete with that. She belittled everything about it and made no effort to fit in. None. Life here with me, with our son, it was never going to be enough. She wanted to keep moving and not waste her life as the wife of a country doctor. She didn't want the whole picket fence.'

Jessica's eyes widened. It was all falling into place and making sense to her. 'And I said the same to you.'

'And you have every right to want more than this town. I would never want you to stay where you don't want to be.'

'That's not why I said what I did. It was nothing to do with this town…or you. It was someone else. Someone I trusted and loved, who lied to me in the worst possible way. He made me believe that we had a future when all along he knew we didn't. He destroyed my belief in men, marriage and commitment. I thought I had my happily ever after and it all fell apart.'

Harrison turned to face her. 'Is that why you don't want to settle in one place for too long?'

Jessica nodded. 'I didn't want to be lied to again. He was married and never told me. I was clueless but discovered he had a family already. A wife and children. Everything I thought we would have, he already had. So I guess I gave up on believing in that dream pretty darn quickly.'

'I'm so sorry that happened to you.'

'I am too because it has scarred me.'

'I hope the bastard pays one day for what he did to you.'

'Not just me, his family as well. His wife knows; she's the one who called me and told me to walk away.'

Harrison shook his head. His expression was filled with compassion she wasn't expecting.

'You deserve better than that, Jessica. So does his wife. Two innocent women were hurt at the hands of one calculating man. He should rot in hell for his actions. What he did is unforgivable and I'm not surprised it made you feel the way you did.'

Jessica was thrown by his words. There was no hint of judgement and she suddenly felt as if a weight lifted. The guilt she had been carrying had flowed into every aspect of her life and this man was somehow taking that away, just by the way he looked at her.

'I felt…responsible. I thought I didn't deserve love after that. I didn't want to get close to someone and have my heart broken because I knew I wouldn't survive it again.'

'And that's what I did. I pulled you close and then I pushed you away,' Harrison said with remorse colouring his voice. 'I'm so sorry. I was a fool.'

'We both had our reasons for what we did and said.'

'I shouldn't have rushed us into what we did that night.' He paused. 'But I couldn't stop myself and, while I'm sorry beyond words for how I hurt you afterwards, I don't regret a minute of it. I was the happiest I have ever been.'

Jessica had to agree with everything he had said. She regretted rushing too, but it was the best night of her life. Suddenly she felt that she finally understood the man sitting beside her. He was the man her heart had led her to believe. Not the man that her past had made her want to think he was.

'After everything I did, everything I put you through, I can't believe you're here—shouldn't you be on a plane, Jessica?'

'I should, but some things are more important than a job.'

'You missed your flight to come back to check up on Bryce?'

'And you.'

'But why? You didn't know any of what I just told you,' he said, not taking his eyes away from her beautiful face. 'You compromised your new role without being sure of anything.'

'I guess I took a leap of faith. I saw the depth of your love for your son; I thought that there had to be a reason for your actions. I thought perhaps you needed your heart to be mended too. And if I was wrong, then I'd have learnt another hard lesson about myself.'

'And here I was thinking that if I kept seeing you I would be the one who would get hurt when you packed up and moved on.'

'I don't want to move on, Harrison. I never

thought I would say it, but I feel at home here...'

'With me?' he cut in.

'Yes, with you.'

The ICU nurse appeared though the swing doors, pulling free her mask. 'I have wonderful news. Bryce has stabilised. His temperature's back down to thirty-six point five. He's breathing unassisted. Your little boy is going to be just fine.'

Harrison jumped to his feet like a man who had been given a new lease on life. But before he raced in to see his son he reached for Jessica's hand. 'Please come in with me. I want to introduce my son to the most amazing woman in the world and the doctor who saved his life.'

'We did it together, Harrison.'

'Yes, we did and I hope it's just the beginning. I want to spend the rest of my life here with you. I want to fall asleep every night with you wrapped in my arms and wake up the same way.'

Jessica didn't try to hide the smile that was born of her uncontained happiness.

'But it's a big ask, Jessica. I'm a country boy

at heart and I want my son to grow up here with his grandparents. But I could commute to see you in Adelaide and you could do the same some weeks maybe, because I don't want you to give up on your dream of being the Head of Paediatrics in Adelaide. That's not fair on you. And I never want you to have to give up something for me and regret that decision...'

'I wouldn't regret anything. I would willingly walk away from that role to be here with you if you're asking me to stay.'

'I am, but...' he said, holding her hand so tightly as if she were his lifeline and he would be hers.

'But nothing—if you want me here then I want to be here more than anything I've ever wanted. And I'd never regret anything,' she promised with tears of happiness welling in her eyes. 'Besides, who says I have to give up on a dream for ever? As the hospital grows I have a feeling there might just be a need for a Head of Paediatrics right here in Armidale.'

Harrison pulled her into his arms and kissed

her as passionately as he had that fateful night
when their worlds changed for ever.

'I love you, Jessica.'

'And I love you, Dr Harrison Wainwright.'

EPILOGUE

'WHAT A STUNNING VIEW.'

'Yes, it is,' Harrison said as he looked across at the silhouette of his beautiful bride.

Her blonde hair was swept to one side with an antique clasp his mother had gifted her new daughter-in-law. It was the *something old.* The neckline of the stunning white satin wedding gown with a lace bodice skimmed her bare shoulders. It was the *something new.* On the table nearby was a small white satin purse that Harrison had recognised the moment he'd seen it. It was the one that Rachel had carried on the day she'd married Harrison's best friend, Sam. He knew it because he had bought it for Rachel as a gift. It was the *something borrowed.* Harrison's gaze dropped to the bracelet that caught the light and sparkled as Jessica moved her wrist. It was a gift from Bryce. With help from his grandfather, he had made a bracelet of azure glass beads for his new mummy. It was the *something blue*.

Harrison did not see the Sydney cityscape; he only had eyes for Jessica. She was everything he could ask for and more and he knew he was the luckiest man in the world. And he was not the only one to consider himself lucky. His family adored her and they'd quickly and warmly welcomed Jessica with open arms.

She turned to face him. 'I guess for that much money you would hope it would be nice,' she laughed.

'Oh, you're talking about what's outside the window,' he said as he crossed the room and pulled her into his arms. 'It was all for a good cause. That auction raised enough for two new dialysis units and will go a long way towards a new wing for the hospital.'

'Well, now we have a baby on the way, you might want to cut back on extravagances like a fifteen-thousand-dollar stay in the big smoke.'

Harrison dropped to his knees and kissed the barely visible bump that would in six months be a new Wainwright.

'I know medical school fees for four of them will cripple us.'

'Four?' she gasped.

'You're right. Between Bryce and this one on the way, we're good for now,' he said, smiling. He loved how easily Jessica had slipped into their lives, how quickly she had formed a bond with Bryce, earning his love and trust in a way that had melted Harrison's heart further.

'Besides,' he said, resuming the thread of their conversation, 'if we have four, maybe not all of them will want to be doctors.'

Jessica laughed as she leant into the strength of her husband's embrace. 'I love you, Harrison Wainwright.'

'I'm glad to hear it because I'm crazy in love with you, Dr Wainwright, and I will spend the rest of my life showing you just how much.'

* * * * *

LET'S TALK

Romance

For exclusive extracts, competitions
and special offers, find us online:

f facebook.com/millsandboon

⊙ @millsandboonuk

🐦 @millsandboon

Or get in touch on 0844 844 1351*

For all the latest titles coming soon,
visit millsandboon.co.uk/nextmonth

*Calls cost 7p per minute plus your phone company's price per
minute access charge

Want even more
ROMANCE?

Join our bookclub today!

'Mills & Boon books, the perfect way to escape for an hour or so.'

Miss W. Dyer

'Excellent service, promptly delivered and very good subscription choices.'

Miss A. Pearson

'You get fantastic special offers and the chance to get books before they hit the shops'

Mrs V. Hall

Visit millsandbook.co.uk/Bookclub and save on brand new books.

MILLS & BOON